THE VAMPIRE'S HEART

The Vampire's Heart

Mark A. Roeder

Writers Club Press
San Jose New York Lincoln Shanghai

The Vampire's Heart

All Rights Reserved © 2002 by Mark A. Roeder

No part of this book may be reproduced or transmitted in any form or by any means, graphic, electronic, or mechanical, including photocopying, recording, taping, or by any information storage retrieval system, without the permission in writing from the publisher.

Writers Club Press
an imprint of iUniverse, Inc.

For information address:
iUniverse, Inc.
5220 S. 16th St., Suite 200
Lincoln, NE 68512
www.iuniverse.com

This book is a work of fiction. Names, characters, places, and incidents are products of the author's imagination, or are used fictionally. Any resemblance to actual events, locales, or persons, living or dead, is entirely coincidental.

All registered trademarks mentioned in this book are the property of their respective owners. No infringement is intended or should be inferred.

ISBN: 0-595-22564-0

Printed in the United States of America

This book is dedicated to all those who feel they don't quite fit in. Without people like us, the world would be a boring place.

Contents

Chronology		*xi*
Introduction		*xiii*
Chapter 1	The Boy from Britain	1
Chapter 2	Mr. Diggory	19
Chapter 3	The Twins and The Wolf	35
Chapter 4	The Ice Thaws at Last	49
Chapter 5	My First "Date"	59
Chapter 6	A Close Brush with Death	69
Chapter 7	Warnings from All Sides	77
Chapter 8	The Vampire at Griswold Jr./Sr. High	91
Chapter 9	Desperate Measures	99
Chapter 10	Into the Vampire's Lair	109
Chapter 11	Josiah's Other Life	125
Chapter 12	A Changed Life	145
Chapter 13	Lurking in the Lair	163
Chapter 14	Death's Doorstep	177
Chapter 15	Josiah and his Son	183
Chapter 16	The End and The Beginning	189
Chapter 17	Homecoming	199
About the Author		*211*

Acknowledgements

I'd like to thank Ken Clark, Jim Hertwig, and John Radez for their wonderful suggestions and help with editing.

Chronology

Spring 1997

Introduction

Even though Graham, the main character of *The Vampire's Heart*, is a boy with questions about his sexual orientation, this novel is not part of my *Gay Youth Chronicles* series. The story is set in a small town not unlike Verona, Indiana (from my other books), but I've left its location vague. It's simply a small community, such as those than can be found anywhere in Indiana, or anywhere in the Midwest for that matter. None of the characters from my other novels have a part to play in this story, although the most famous of them is mentioned.

CHAPTER 1

The Boy from Britain

I walked through the darkness, threading my way through the trees as a steady rain fell down upon me. There was only a slight chill in the air, but I shivered in my soaked shirt and wet jeans. I was cold. Even my boxers were wet and clung to my skin. I was miserable, but my physical discomfort was the least reason for it.

I sat cross-legged at the base of a giant oak and bowed my head as the rain dripped upon me from the branches and leaves above. My shoulders shuddered as I began to cry. My hot tears warmed my cheeks as they fell to mingle with the rain.

I was so tired of feeling lonely. I was so tired of being alone. There was not a single boy I could call a friend. More sobs welled up from my chest; another sign of my weakness. I was the shortest, skinniest, puniest boy in my entire class. I was pathetic. I was better off dead.

With trembling hands I withdrew the bottle from my pocket. I screwed off the lid and looked down at enough sleeping pills to put me asleep forever. I was tired of being friendless and alone. Thirteen years was enough. I was determined that this would be my last, lonely, miserable night.

I raised the bottle to my lips with an unsteady hand, but a loud hoot and the flap of wings startled me and I spilled the pills all over the ground. I looked up to see a tawny owl peered down at me from a branch above, eyes blinking.

"Thanks a lot. Look what you've done."

The owl didn't answer, she just looked at me and blinked. I knew her. She visited me often and I'd named her Angelica. I first came upon her early that spring. I was sitting under the very same oak tree I was now, writing in my journal, and there she was, as unafraid as if I were one of her kind. That didn't surprise me greatly, I had a way with animals. I was one of them and some would even come when I called. Since our first meeting, Angelica searched me out when I was in the forest. It was a rare time when she did not find me.

"Did you bring me any secrets tonight?" I asked her as she stared at me. "I'm sure you know plenty."

I almost felt as if she could answer. I'd learned early on there was little difference between fantasy and reality and I allowed them to mix freely when I was alone. It made me less afraid, and less lonely. Sometimes, I pretended I was with friends, especially when I was in the forest. We'd be exploring and they'd be just out of sight all around me. I felt a little safer then, even though it was only pretend. Tonight, however, there was nothing that could help me. I felt more alone than I ever had before. I was beyond help.

"Nothing, huh? It's just as well," I said. Angelica just sat there and kept blinking at me as the rain fell down upon us both. She hooted loudly, just once, then stared at me again.

I looked at the muddy forest floor. Small, white pills were laying all over the fallen leaves. I grew angry.

"Just go away and leave me alone!" I yelled at Angelica, but she just kept staring at me, blinking every now and then. She could act so superior sometimes.

I searched the ground on hands and knees for the pills I'd spilled, scooping them back into the bottle, picking out bits of dead leaves. I was truly a loser. I couldn't even do myself in properly.

As I picked up the pills, now one by one, I felt fright tingling up my spine. I didn't know why, but fear seized me. A dog howled not far away, setting the hair on the back of my neck on end, and Angelica flying off in the night. I leaped to my feet and peered through the inky darkness, but saw nothing. Only silence filled my ears, but something was there. I could *feel* it. My heart thumped in my chest, beating wildly as if I'd just finished a long run.

I stood there in stillness, peering into the gloom, squinting to see through the rain. Slowly, a great, dark shape became discernable in the shadows. It grew nearer. It was unlike any dog I'd seen. It was black as night and moved with stealth and grace. I shook from head to foot in terror, but could not bring myself to take my eyes from it. As it drew ever closer I could see its eyes; steel blue, cold, and piercing. I could tell it was no dog at all. There was but one thing it could be—a wolf.

I didn't stop to ponder on what such a creature was doing in the woods; wolves hadn't existed in the wilds of Indiana for nearly two hundred years. I was in too great a terror. As I gaped at it, my hand turned and I dumped all my pills onto the ground once more. The wolf quickened its pace as it bore down upon me. I stood there rooted to the spot as if I had become an oak tree myself. I screwed my eyes shut as the wolf made a great lunge. This was it. This was how I would die. I knew I'd feel its paws upon my chest in a moment and then its teeth on my neck. But—nothing. It was gone.

I opened my eyes, somewhat amazed to find myself in one piece. I was quite whole, however, and there was no sign of the creature that had given me such terror. It was gone as quickly as it had come and left behind only questions.

The wood seemed more frightening than it had before. It had long been the one place I didn't feel afraid, but something had entered it that did not belong there. It seemed as if something were lurking behind every tree and hiding in every shadow.

I stood there as the rain streamed down my face. I forgot about the pills lying in the mud. I forgot my misery and why I had come into the forest. I was too terrified to be lonely or depressed. I was too frightened to die.

I turned toward home and forced myself not to run. If I ran, I was almost certain something would chase me. Perhaps I was being foolish, but my surroundings felt dream-like. I was often chased in my dreams, and the terror of it was in the running. As long as I could keep from bolting, I'd be safe, but if I so much as jogged, the demons of my dreams would be after me. My feet ached to run, but I made them walk. I felt as if I were watched from every side.

My breath was coming hard and fast, even though I was only walking. I tried to calm myself and steady my breathing. I reminded myself that there was nothing in the darkness that was not there in the light. For some reason, the thought did not comfort me.

I screamed as I heard movement nearby. Quick as lightning, something sprang at me and knocked me to the ground. I scrambled to my feet all in a panic and bolted. I could run as fast as anything. My one talent was running, probably because I was forced to do it so very often.

It was not the wolf that pounced on me, but something quite as dangerous. I ran as if my life depended on it.

"Ah get him, Jay, you loser!"

"You were closer!"

I heard them nearly on my heels. I didn't dare to turn around. I knew they'd be on me in a second if I did. It was the neighbor boys, Clay and Jay. They were sixteen year old, sandy-haired twins, who lived for little more than making my life a living hell. They were bullies and I was their favorite punching bag. They were three years older, more than a foot taller, and far more muscular that I. Either one of them picking on me would not have been fair, but they nearly always traveled together. I had no idea what they were doing lurking around in the dark, but I was sure they were up to no good.

I didn't give it a great deal of thought. I was far too busy running for my life. I knew I'd be in for it if they caught me. Exactly what they did to me depended on their mood, but it was never fun. It could range anywhere from rubbing my face in the mud to giving me a black eye and a bloody nose. I wasn't going to experience any of it if I could help it.

The twins began to drop behind. Even with their longer legs I could outrun them. It was probably thanks to them that I could run so very fast. When the twins appeared, my only choices were to outrun them or get knocked around, and I much preferred to outdistance them. The night was a disappointment for the twins—I made it to the safety of my own yard. I could hear them huffing and puffing as they stood on the road glaring at me, but they didn't draw closer. They turned and walked on up the road to their own home.

I went straight to my room, pulled off all my wet clothes and climbed under the covers. My teeth were chattering, partly from the cold, but mostly from fear. I thought that wolf was going to kill me. When it leaped, I just knew it was going to pounce on me and rip me to shreds. I could still see those steel blues eyes staring at me. The fear of the wolf was still in my heart, even though I was safe in my little bed.

Oddly enough, the wolf I thought was going to slay me had kept me from killing myself. I was moments from downing an entire bottle of pills when it caused me to scatter them everywhere. When Angelica made me drop them, they mainly landed on the wet leaves, but when the wolf leaped, I threw them all over the place and most of them landed in the mud. They were ruined.

I guess the wolf had saved my life. I'd gone into the woods to end it all, but now I wasn't so sure I was ready to die. Death was pretty final after all. If I did myself in, I couldn't undo it later if I decided it was a mistake. What was I thinking anyway? How could I do that to my parents, and to Kelly, my only real friend. That was the trouble when I got all depressed, upset, and lonely. I didn't think straight. It was like I wasn't even me. I'd never actually tried to kill myself before, but I'd come close. It was like I was out of my head when I was like that. Sometimes the pain in my life just became too much to handle and I snapped. That's what had happened tonight. I was so lonely that I just couldn't take it anymore.

Tears rolled down my cheeks. I was afraid, but not of the wolf this time, or the twins. I was afraid of myself. How long would it be before I lost it again? Maybe next time, I would kill myself. That thought is what scared me. I knew that when I got all upset that I might do it. And next time, I doubted that a wolf would be there to stop me. Something had to change. I couldn't let my life go on as it had. I desperately needed to end my loneliness.

I sighed. I was thirteen and I'd never been on a date. I guess it wasn't that unusual. Maybe I was a bit young for dating. But I had a fear that nothing would change as I got older. In three years, I'd be sixteen and still dateless. In ten years, I'd be twenty-three and still all by myself. I knew I was doomed. It would have been bad enough if I liked girls, but I'd known for a while that I didn't. It was other boys that got me excited and that made things a thousand times more difficult.

Even if I had been looking for a girlfriend, none of the girls at school would've wanted me. I was small for my age, and thin…a little shrimp. There were boys in my class who already had muscles…and hair sprouting on their chest. I had neither. I looked like a little kid. I wasn't just a kid anymore, though. I wanted to date…to kiss a boy. Finding a girl would've been hard. Finding a boy was impossible. Even if I could tell by looking which ones were like me, which ones were—gay; I'd never have the courage to approach them. If I did, they'd just shoot me down. Who'd want a puny little boy when they could have someone with a man's body?

I sure couldn't approach a guy without knowing if he was gay or not. That was suicide. I got my ass kicked enough without anyone finding out I was gay. If that got out, my life would quickly become a living hell. I'd be dead meat. Every boy at school was bigger and stronger than me and they'd all have it in for me then. There's no way I could let 'em find out about me. The only way I could survive was to remain hidden. Mine was truly a lost cause. If I couldn't reveal myself, what chance did I have of finding someone? Yeah. I was doomed to be alone, at least as far as a boyfriend was concerned. Maybe I could at least find a friend. That'd be better than nothing…way better.

※ ※ ※

They got me the next day of course, the twins that is. There was no real escape from them. They bore down upon me in the hallway, each smashing into me as they passed. It was like being knocked about by two boulders. My books and papers went flying everywhere and the twins laughed as they moved on.

"Ohhhh, that wasn't nice at all," said Kelly.

"Who ever accused the twins of being nice?" I asked her crossly.

"I've seen them be nice."

"Yes—*to girls*. They are almost always nice to girls."

"Not to me."

"You're different."

"Well, thank you very much, Graham Granger," said Kelly putting her hands on her hips. If she hadn't looked so angry, I would have laughed. She looked comical standing there like that.

"I just mean you're too young, and they know you're my friend."

"Sometimes, I wish I were older," she said. "They are quite handsome, aren't they?"

I rolled my eyes.

"Evil is what they are," I said.

"Oh, Graham, how can you say that? No one is evil."

"Then they are about as close as you can get, and you're in love with them! Ha!"

"I am not in love with them. I just said I thought they were handsome."

"And that you wished you were older. What's that about, huh?"

Kelly quickly changed the subject. I let her. I wasn't in the mood to talk about the twins. As far as I was concerned, the less said about them, the better.

I smiled at Kelly as we walked to class. I couldn't do much but smile. It was hard getting a word in with Kelly most of the time. She liked to talk more than anyone I knew. Perhaps that's why she didn't have many friends. Perhaps they found her as annoying as I did sometimes. There were times I wanted to scream *Please stop talking!* at her, but I didn't because I knew how it would hurt her feelings. Besides, I didn't want to lose her.

I frowned. I didn't have many friends either. Kelly was the only one really. There was Mrs. Barrett, who ran the school bookstore. Sometimes I hung out and looked at erasers and stuff while I talked to her. Then there was Eddie, the custodian. I didn't really talk to him much, but we always said "hi" when we passed each other in the halls. Mrs. Riley, who worked in the lunch line, was always nice to me too. She never failed to ask how I was doing and usually gave me a bigger serving of dessert than anyone else. None of them were really friends, though. I didn't have anyone my own age to hang out with—no one to go to the movies with me, or the mall, or anything like that.

I liked Kelly, but it would have been nice to have a guy as a friend. I wasn't one of the "cool" boys at school, so it was difficult. I was small for my age. I was puny and I knew it. I wasn't picked last for teams without reason. I couldn't quite manage to get the basketball up to the basket. I couldn't knock a baseball very far at all. Most of the time I couldn't even hit the ball with the bat. I should have been good at soccer, because I was such a good runner, but I couldn't quite manage to control the ball. I was completely useless for football, except maybe as the water boy. It made me an outcast.

The truth was, there wasn't much I wanted more than a friend, another boy I could talk to about guy stuff. Kelly was a good friend, but there are just certain things you can't say to a girl. Kelly also had no interest at all in horror movies, monsters, and other guy things that I wanted to talk about. I made the mistake of showing her one of my monster magazines once and she told me it was "sick". Hearing her say that made my chest feel funny. I could tell she thought I was stupid for being interested in anything like that.

"I do think she'd look better if her hair were shorter," said Kelly.

I realized I'd drifted off and had no idea what she was talking about. From what little I caught at the end, I think it was a good thing. The doorway to English loomed before us, so I was spared further discussion of whoever's hair.

At lunch, my eyes locked on a boy I'd never seen before. He stood out for two reasons. First, he was sitting all to himself, and second, he didn't look quite like anyone I'd ever seen before. I couldn't quite put my finger on it, but there was something very different about him.

I wasn't the only one who noticed him. The girls sitting with Kelly had already picked him out.

"I heard he's from England. Tess heard him speak and said he has the most beautiful British accent."

"And what dreamy eyes," said Shelly.

I had to fight hard not to roll my eyes. I did it too often as it was. Kelly often punched me in the shoulder for it. I couldn't help it sometimes. One disadvantage of having a girl for a best friend was that I usually had to sit with girls. It's not that I had anything against them; it's just that listening to them talk sometimes made me want to hurl. I had to silently agree with Shelly, however…his eyes were dreamy.

I was relieved when Bry Hartnett sat near and said, "You can't be talking about the British freak."

Bry was captain of the football team. He was a jock with a major attitude. His motto was "If it's not happening to me, it doesn't matter." He could be a real jerk and at times I despised him. At other times I dreamed about him. Something drew me to him, despite his attitude, or perhaps because of it. He was so confident and self-assured. He was sixteen or seventeen, but he seemed all grown up to me. He probably even shaved.

I was glad Bry had arrived. The conversation would definitely be more interesting and I could feast my eyes upon him as he sat there. I never missed an opportunity to look him over. He looked so good in his class jacket. And, he had muscles. Yum.

Bry did not amuse Shelly at all. She shot a wicked glare at him, but he only smiled. He didn't care what she thought. He had dozens of girls like her after him and he knew it. He was *Mr. Popularity* at school and loved (or at least envied) by all.

Some of the girls were as unhappy with Bry as Shelly, others looked at him adoringly. I sat there with mixed emotions. Part of me felt like gazing at Bry adoringly too, although I just knew he'd kick my ass for it if he caught me. Another part of me was jealous of those girls. At least they had a chance with him, especially if they were willing to put out. I didn't know anything for sure, but I'd heard that Bry had had lots of girls. If I was a girl…I didn't let myself go further. I didn't want to be a girl. I was so small and slim that some people treated me like I was one and I didn't like it.

An argument broke out among the girls as to the new boy's best features. I kind of liked listening to them, but it only increased my jealousy. It made me more uncomfortable, too. I could hardly stand sitting there. Before I knew what I was doing, I had stood, picked up my tray, and walked toward the boy sitting alone.

I'm not quite sure what made me do it, but I had an overpowering desire to escape from the table of yakking girls and an overwhelming pity for the boy sitting all by himself. I knew what it was like to be an outsider. It's not as if no one would talk to me or anything, but I was so small that I think people often just didn't realize I was there.

I still couldn't believe I was bold enough to approach him. It wasn't like me at all. The boy was cute, however, and I liked him, even though I didn't know him. I wanted a friend, maybe even a boyfriend, and so I kept going until I was standing in front of him. Having the courage to go so far made me feel like I'd just swam the English Channel.

"Mind if I sit?" I asked.

The boy looked at me. His expression was curious, neither inviting nor unfriendly. I got the feeling he'd rather not have me there, but he didn't protest. I sat down across from him with my tray.

"I'm Graham."

"Josiah," he said in a clipped tone. It was as if he wanted to make the word as short as possible to avoid speaking to me. I could detect the British accent that the girls were going on about. I could see what they meant. It was sexy.

I got a good look at Josiah while I was sitting so close. His hair was jet black, as black as it could possibly be, and his eyes were blue. His pale skin made his hair look that much darker close up. His features were finely drawn and yet he exuded an aura of strength. He was cute, and even beautiful in a mysterious, powerful sort of way. Even though he was wearing a long-sleeved shirt I could tell he had a slim, solid build, not the bulging muscular football type, like Bry, but compact and firm. The sight of him made me breathe just a little harder.

"You new here?"

"Yes."

"It's tough being new, hard to make friends and all that," I said.

"Yes." He said it as if he didn't really care. Josiah was certainly a queer boy. I sighed. If only he *was* queer.

An uneasy silence followed. I observed Josiah as I picked at my green beans. He kept his arms close against his body. It was like he was trying to take up as little space as possible to avoid detection. He didn't appear nervous in the least, but he carefully avoided eye contact with anyone who walked by. Several girls were trying to catch his eye, but it wasn't happening. Some guys were eyeing him too, although not with dreamy looks on their faces. Josiah ignored them completely. It was almost as if he were all alone, even though he was surrounded by others.

I wanted to strike up a conversation with him, but it wasn't easy, especially with his one-word answers to my questions. I wasn't exactly the outgoing type myself. Okay, I wasn't the outgoing type at all, and that made it harder still. It was difficult for me to carry any conversation. I usually listened more than talked.

"I have to go," said Josiah and quickly departed after only a few minutes.

That was it. All I got out of him was six words. There was something that intrigued me about him. He didn't seem eager to make friends, but I had a feeling he needed one, and badly. In those brief moments when I'd glimpsed his eyes I read a certain yearning there. It wasn't a sexual yearning, like I'm sure often showed in my own, but a deep, yet simple yearning that seemed to call out *Save me.* Yeah, there was no doubt Josiah needed a buddy. I needed one too. I was more than tired of being virtually friendless. I knew I could be a good friend. Josiah needed a friend, I just knew it, and that friend was going to be me. It was out of character for me to be so determined about something, but it seemed the day for that. It wasn't like me, but I was resolute nonetheless.

🍁　　　🍁　　　🍁

I walked home after school. I lived far enough out of town that I could have taken the school bus, but the twins rode it and it was worth any effort to avoid even a few minutes with them. It was difficult for them to beat on me with the bus driver watching, but they were nearly as good at verbal abuse as they were physical. I didn't enjoy all the names they'd come up with it to hurl at me, like *girly-boy*, *runt*, *pansy*, and *stick boy*. They loved to point out that I was small and weak. Riding on the bus was *not* fun. Besides, it wasn't a long walk home and I rather enjoyed it. I loved being in the forest and I nearly always cut through it when returning from school. I felt at peace there.

I didn't go straight home. Instead, I walked to my favorite oak tree, the one where I'd discovered Angelica. I slipped off my backpack and pulled out my journal. I spent a lot of time alone in the woods, sitting under that tree. That's where I did my best thinking, and all my writing in my journal—most of it anyway.

Most of the time, I just sat under my tree and thought, while I enjoyed the peace of the forest. Thinking allowed me to organize my thoughts and make them make sense. When I had them down in my mind, I wrote them in my journal. It was filled with my thoughts and feelings. It held all my secrets.

I thought about Bry. He was *gorgeous*. It almost didn't seem possible that he could be so handsome. If that wasn't enough; there was his body. He had broad shoulders and big, bulging biceps. I spent a lot of time imagining what he looked like without a shirt. It made me breathe funny. Sometimes, I sat under my tree and fantasized about wrestling with Bry. Almost always, he took his shirt off in my fantasies. I loved imagining what his chest looked like. I knew it must be muscular. He probably had hard abs too.

For a while, my thoughts had disturbed me. I knew I was supposed to be thinking about girls instead of boys, but then Mom had *the* talk with me, the talk about sex. I was expecting that talk to come from Dad, but he didn't want to touch it. I even asked Mom why he wasn't talking to me about it, but she got all nervous and made me promise not to tell him she'd talked to me about it. She seemed afraid. I guess I shouldn't have been surprised. Dad wasn't an ideal father. He wasn't bad or anything, but he yelled sometimes. We got on well, mostly, but I know he wanted me to be a big football stud like Bry, and that wasn't going to happen. I knew I was a disappointment to him.

Most of the talk embarrassed the hell out of me and Mom both, but I learned some things that really helped. One thing I learned is that boys my ages often had a kind of hero worship for boys like Bry. Some boys even experimented sexually with other boys, even though they ended up dating girls. And then there was what Mom told me about Uncle Rob. Uncle Rob was in his thirties and wasn't married. I've never thought much about it, but I'd never so much as heard about him dating a girl. Mom told me why and warned me to *never* mention it to Dad. Uncle Rob was gay. It kind of shocked me, but it made things easier. Uncle Rob was my favorite uncle and was the coolest guy I knew. If he was gay, then it must be okay. I knew my Mom and her brother were close. Mom didn't seem to care if Rob was gay or not. I had the feeling that if I told Mom I was gay, that she'd be okay with it. That was a big weight off my shoulders because I was becoming pretty sure I was gay. I wasn't so sure about Dad. He hated Uncle Rob and I'd never been able to figure out why. Dad also seemed to want to keep me away from my uncle. Maybe it was because he was gay. Maybe he thought Uncle Rob would make me gay too, or something. That was a pretty stupid idea, but it seemed to fit with my dad's way of thinking. Uncle Rob lived really far away, so I didn't get to see him much. I was beginning to wish he were closer so we could talk about a few things.

I wondered about some of the things Mom said. I also wondered why she brought up the subject of being gay. Did she suspect me? Was there something about me that was tipping her off? She never came right out and asked me, but there was something in her eyes…an unspoken question—*Are you like Uncle Rob?*

I thought about the hero worship thing. I think my feelings for Bry were more than that. There was definitely some hero worship there—Bry was tall and built and athletic and handsome. There was more to it, though. Sometimes I caught myself looking at his butt and at the bulge in his jeans. I didn't really know quite what I wanted to do with Bry, but I think it was sexual. In my fantasies, we just wrestled, but I sure liked rubbing up against his sexy body. When I'd thought about him for a while, I got excited, it made me hard. The first time I ever masturbated, I was thinking about Bry. I was a virgin, but I knew he excited me.

Josiah, the new boy, excited me too, but not in quite the same way as Bry. I was drawn to Bry because of his cocky attitude and his muscles. I was drawn to Josiah because he was dark and mysterious. He didn't have a muscular body like Bry, but there was something about him that was irresistibly sexy. It wasn't really Josiah's looks that attracted me. Rather, it was my need for a friend. Josiah seemed so sad and lonely. I thought maybe he needed a friend too. Then again, he was kind of cute. He'd probably make a good boyfriend. Maybe he'd be sweet and kind. I didn't think I was ready for a boyfriend, but who knew?

I wrote my feelings down in my journal. I was glad I knew that Mom was cool with her brother being gay. It made me feel like she'd accept me if I told her I was gay too. I wasn't completely sure if I was, but the evidence was mounting. I didn't really care for girls and when I thought of guys like Bry...Mmmmmm. I was glad I knew about Uncle Rob, too. It made me feel better about myself. If I did turn out to be gay, and I thought I probably would, then knowing Uncle Rob was gay would make me feel better. I could probably even talk to him about stuff on the phone.

I'd been sitting under my tree for over an hour. I knew it was time to go. My parents didn't mind if I was a little late. They knew I liked to mess around in the woods and they always encourage me to be outdoors—like maybe it would build me up and I wouldn't be so puny. They'd get worried if I was too late, though, so I had to watch how much time I spent under my tree.

Just as I was getting ready to leave, Angelica landed on a branch above me. I was a little surprised. I saw her often in the woods, but it was usually later in the evening, or at night.

"There you are," I said. "I was just leaving, but I'm glad you came to say *hi*."

Angelica looked at me and slightly bowed her head. I smiled at her and went on my way.

🍁 🍁 🍁

I walked in to find the house quiet—no surprise there. My dad had his nose stuck in the newspaper in the living room. He said "Hello, Graham", as I passed with barely a pause in his reading. Dad had his face hidden behind a paper so often that I wasn't quite sure what he looked like. My mother pinched my cheeks as I walked through the kitchen and picked up a cookie. I hated having my cheeks pinched, but it wasn't so bad a price to pay for the cookies my mom always kept on hand. There was always a big plate of them on the table that never seemed to empty: chocolate chip, oatmeal with pecans, and chewy coconut.

I made the mistake of pausing too long and Mom pinched my cheeks again and added a "You are such a cute little boy". I rolled my eyes and ducked away before she could have another go at my cheeks. For some reason, all the females of my family, aunts, cousins, and all, felt compelled to pinch my cheeks. I think it had something to do with me being small. I was thirteen, but they often seemed to think I was five. It infuriated me.

My parents weren't bad as parents go, but sometimes they seemed like they'd just stepped out from some old black and white sitcom. Dad never seemed to do anything except go to work and read the paper and Mom was forever baking something. I had more than a sneaking suspicion that they weren't my real parents. I'd always felt that way, but then again they had been my parents for as long as I could remember. The thing that really made me suspicious is that

Dad had jet-black hair and black eyes, while my hair was so light blond it was practically white and my eyes were blue. Mom had auburn hair and brown eyes. I had no brothers or sisters, so I had no one for comparison, but I didn't see how my blond hair could come from black and auburn. Perhaps it had something to do with recessive genes or something—we'd studied genes in school—Mendel's peas and stuff like that. I didn't even have any blond uncles or aunts either, so that made me suspect I wasn't one of them at all—not that the thought bothered me. It would've been a relief to find out I was adopted or something.

I escaped from further cheek pinching, but before I could even make it to the stairs, my dad called out to me.

"Graham, I found an ad here you might want to see."

I turned on my heel and headed for the living room. I'd been trying to find an afternoon or weekend job to earn a little money. I was thirteen and was beginning to think about the day I could drive. Three years was an exceptionally long time, but cars were expensive. If I wanted to have any chance at all of getting one, even a lousy used junker, I needed to start saving for it as soon as possible. So far I'd had no luck. My only prospect was a job flipping burgers at minimum wage and even that glamorous career seemed beyond my reach. No one wanted me. They all seemed to think I was a little kid. Sometimes I felt like that whole world was stacked against me because of my age. It was age discrimination, pure and simple, but no one cared.

Dad handed me a section of the paper. I could tell he really wanted me to find a job because normally no one touched the paper but him. He acted like it was made of gold or something.

I looked down the column of ads until my eyes lit on the one Dad had pointed out. "Wanted: Boy to do yard work and run errands. Good pay, hours negotiable. Must be dependable. Apply in-person at 825 West County Road."

It sounded like just what I was looking for. What's more, it wasn't far from home. I memorized the address and gave Dad back his paper. He carefully put the section back in its place, like a fussy librarian putting a book back on the shelf. I smiled; I might have just found a job at last.

CHAPTER 2

Mr. Diggory

The next day after school, I dropped off my books at home, combed my hair, and set off for 825 West County Road. It was less than a mile away, but I'd never been there in my entire life. I'd been down the road, of course, but not up the long lane that led to the address. I turned onto the lane and still had a bit of a walk before I reached the house. It was a long, low structure that faced away from the lane. I walked around the front to find a beautiful little house with lots of windows and a porch running along the entire length. There were lots of trees and a great many odd plants growing in the yard that gradually disappeared into the woods.

Two little dogs began yapping and barking even before I made it to the big glass double door. A man soon appeared who looked as if he could be anywhere from fifty to eighty something. He had long white hair, kind brown eyes, and was tall and slim. He motioned for me to wait a moment while he quieted the dogs and made his way out onto the porch.

"Basil Diggory, at your service. How can I help you, young man?"

He struck me as a bit odd, but he was friendly and smiled at me as if he were very pleased indeed to see me. Before I had a chance to answer, he spoke again.

"Come about the job I see. Well, you are just the boy I'm looking for I'm sure. I've been expecting you."

He looked at me with an appraising eye and an air of recognition. I'd never seen him before, however, which was odd, considering that everyone knew everyone in our small community.

"I'm Graham," I said.

"Of course you are and glad to meet you. You may call me Basil." He shook my hand most vigorously. "But I'm being rude, have a seat and I'll get us some tea."

Before I had a chance to say a word he had whisked inside and was back in a flash with two steaming cups of tea. I took a seat in one of the many rocking chairs on the porch.

"Hope you like English Breakfast. Rather fond of it myself any time of day. Yes, that's just the thing," he said as he took a sip.

I took a sip as well and found I rather liked it, although I'd never cared that much for tea before. I took another sip as I sat there, trying to gather my wits about me. Basil had quite an overpowering personality, although I found myself liking him quite a lot. He smiled a great deal and seemed always on the verge of laughing at some joke.

"About the job…" I said.

"Oh yes," he said, putting down his tea. "I need someone to mow the lawn, pull weeds out of the flower beds, keep the plants watered, run errands, that sort of thing. Think you can handle that?"

"Certainly," I said, "but there, uh, doesn't seem to be much yard here."

"True enough!" he said laughing. "It is a rather small yard, but quite sufficient. The plants take a good deal of tending, however. When you aren't taking care of that you'll be running errands for me, mainly picking up packages and that sort of thing, groceries and the like. I'm extremely busy and don't have time to go running about town all the time."

"Sounds good," I said. I wanted to ask him how much I'd get paid, but I thought he might consider it rude. He took another sip of tea and looked into my eyes as if he could read my mind.

"I'll be happy to pay you, say, eight dollars an hour? That sound fair?"

"Yes sir!" I said, failing to hide the enthusiasm in my voice. It was about twice what I was expecting. That car might be mine after all.

"You needn't call me *sir*, "Basil" will be just fine. I can use you a couple of hours or so most afternoons after school and a few hours on the weekends when you can spare them. I'm sure you're a busy boy, so we'll try and work around your schedule. No work on Fridays as I know boys like yourself like to go out then. If you want more hours than that, I'm sure I can find you something to do."

I took another sip of tea, which I was really beginning to like. It all sounded almost too good to be true. Basil's enthusiasm was contagious. I found myself wanting to start work right then.

"You can start tomorrow," he said as if he knew my thoughts. "Right now, I'll introduce you to the boys. Don't worry, they are quite friendly and won't bite. You might have some trouble in keeping them off you, however. They simply love visitors. They'll calm down when they get used to you, but at first you can expect quite a greeting."

He opened the front door and the two little dogs that had had their faces pressed to the glass the entire time came bounding out. They jumped into my lap. I had to sit my tea down quickly to avoid dumping it all over myself.

"The Yorkie is Taylor and the very furry one, the Shih Tzu, is Devon. Calm down, boys!"

Taylor and Devon were licking all over my face and pawing at me. I stroked their hair and scratched them behind the ears, which they thoroughly enjoyed. Taylor fell onto his back in my lap and looked at me with intelligent eyes. He seemed to be saying, "What are you waiting for?" I scratched his belly and he squirmed with pleasure. Devon licked my face so much he was getting me wet.

In just a couple of minutes the two little dogs were calmly sitting on my lap while I petted them both.

"I'd say you've made two new friends," laughed Basil.

I smiled at him. He was the friendliest adult I'd ever met. Something about him just put me at ease and made me feel that I belonged. I think what I liked best about him was that he didn't treat me like a little kid. I could tell he was someone who would never make a move to pinch my cheeks.

There was a loud poof and smoke billowed out an open window. Basil jumped to his feet and ran in the house. He was back mere moments later.

"Too late. That's one pot I should have been watching."

"Is everything okay?" I asked. A rather large amount of smoke had come out of the house.

"Oh yes, it's quite ruined of course, but no real harm done. I do need to get back to work, however, or another pot will be doing the same. Come by tomorrow after school and you can start work. I'll have some packages for you to pick up and we'll go from there."

I stood up and the little dogs jumped to the deck.

"I'll be here! Goodbye, Basil. And goodbye, Taylor and Devon."

"Until tomorrow," said Basil. He swept back inside, his little dogs nipping at his heels and barking loudly.

I felt very light as I walked home. I had a feeling that I'd really like my new job. I certainly liked Basil and his little dogs. Basil did seem kind of peculiar, but in a good way, not bad. He certainly wasn't like any other adult I'd ever met. I couldn't put my finger on it, but there was something definitely different about him. Whatever it was, I liked it, so I guess it didn't really matter that I couldn't figure it out.

🍁   🍁   🍁

I was still thinking about my new job when I got up the next morning. Dad actually dipped his paper for a moment and gave me a quick smile as he sat at the kitchen table. I knew that meant he was proud of me for going out and getting a job. I smeared strawberry jam on my toast and ate it while wondering what it would be like to work for Basil. It would sure beat flipping burgers in any case.

At school, I could hardly pull my mind away from my new job and found it hard to concentrate on what my teachers were saying. Of course that wasn't surprising. I usually found it hard to pay attention in class. Nothing my teachers were saying seemed all that important to me, although they seemed to think my life would end if I didn't learn what they had to teach. I doubted it.

I kept an eye out for Josiah, but I didn't see him until mid-morning. Doreen Simple was pestering him at his locker and he didn't seem pleased in the least. He was giving her the same clipped answers to questions as he had given me the day before and was inviting no conversation. He was not impolite in the least, but he gave her no encouragement whatsoever. I could tell she was greatly disappointed. She was biting her lip as she walked away and looked as if she were about to cry. No doubt she had a crush on Josiah. Many of the girls seemed to have a crush on him. He was the constant topic of Kelly and her friends.

When Doreen turned away from Josiah, I detected a look of sadness in his eyes. I didn't understand it, but it was clearly there. He turned and looked at me. I felt very uncomfortable. I hoped he didn't think I was spying on him, although I guess I was in a way. I had no time to think about it. I caught sight of the twins coming down the hallway and ducked out of sight before they could see me.

At lunch, Kelly was whispering to me as Mrs. Riley ladled something that could have been creamed corn onto my tray. Her whispers were all about Josiah. I was slightly annoyed, but she was giving me some new information about him, such as his last name—Huntington.

"Go sit with him again and see what you can find out," whispered Kelly as we left the cafeteria line. "You're a boy; he'll be more likely to tell you things."

I could just imagine the type of things she wanted me to find out for her. I had my own plans, however, and, for the moment, they traveled in the same direction as those of Kelly. If she thought I was sitting with him to get information for her, then so much the better.

Josiah was sitting alone again. I walked over to him with a faint sense of fear and sat down.

"Hey, Josiah."

"Hello," he said.

It was the same as the day before. I struggled to make conversation, and Josiah said little. I felt that he didn't want me there, but he didn't tell me to go away. Perhaps he was too polite, but just maybe, I thought, he liked not having to sit there all alone with eyes peering at him. There were plenty of eyes peering at him too. He had quickly become the mysterious boy that all the girls adored. Some of the boys were looking at him as well. They seemed jealous of the attention he was getting, especially since he didn't seem to want it, or even acknowledge it. I'd heard some of them mumbling about Josiah thinking he was better than everyone else. I didn't get that feeling from him at all. He didn't act superior in the least. He seemed more like someone who wanted to reach out to others, but didn't quite know how. Perhaps I was wrong, however. If Josiah was seeking the company of others, then why didn't he make some effort to meet those that approached him half-way? He was definitely going to be a tough nut to crack.

I saw Bry Hartnett eye Josiah coldly as he passed. Most likely he didn't like the fact that someone was taking attention away from him. He was quite accustomed to being the main attraction. Most of the girls had a crush on him, and most of the boys wanted to be him, or just be with him. He had a lot of hangers-on, mainly boys who hoped to gain some type of popularity just by being associated with him. I thought that was rather pathetic myself, although even I was tempted. It might be nice to be popular for once.

Josiah never ate much. He picked at his food, in much the same way I picked at mine, and his tray seemed nearly untouched when he was done. I didn't need to eat a lot, because I was small, but I wondered about him. Josiah was a lot bigger than me.

Lunch was soon over and all I'd learned was that Josiah had recently moved from Georgia. He said he'd lived there for nearly ten years. That didn't seem to make much sense. If it were so, then he'd have been living there since he was about five, but he had no trace of a southern accent. If he'd said he'd just moved from London, I'd have believed him without doubt, but Georgia seemed unlikely. I wondered if he was just making up things because he thought I was nosy.

My heart beat a little faster when I was near Josiah. I don't know if it was the excitement of possibly having a friend at last, or if it was something more. I thought about Josiah a lot. I wanted to be with him. I just couldn't figure out if it was because I wanted him as a friend or a boyfriend. I'd given lots and lots of thought to having a good friend who was a boy, but I'd never really thought all that much about having a boyfriend. I wasn't even positive I was interested in boys that way (although I was pretty sure), but there was something about Josiah. I sighed. I was confused about so many things.

Kelly seemed happy enough with what information I gave her after lunch. It made me feel a little like a spy, but I wasn't exactly telling secrets. That I would not do. I was going to be careful, however. I wasn't going to screw up my plans (as uncertain as they were) so that Kelly and those giggling girls could learn something about their dream boy.

❦   ❦   ❦

It was a beautiful afternoon and I enjoyed the walk to Basil's house. It was spring and the plants and leaves seemed to be getting a bit greener every day. I loved trees, and all other plants, for that matter. Just taking a stroll as I was doing brought me an immense amount of enjoyment. I'd learned to take pleasure in little things long ago. My family wasn't exactly poor, but we sure weren't wealthy. My parents couldn't afford to buy me a lot of stuff like video games and computers and CD players like most of the other kids got. It wasn't so bad really. If I could have as much fun walking through the trees as others could playing their video games, well then I was okay.

I was at my destination before I knew it. I couldn't even remember walking up the little lane. I knocked on the door and Basil Diggory motioned me in.

"No need to knock, Graham, you'll be in and out of here all the time from now on, at least until you get sick of me. Now, before we start, have a cup of tea."

I was quickly learning that hot tea was somewhat of a trademark for Basil. The day before we'd had English Breakfast and today he presented me with a steaming cup of Black Currant. It tasted a bit tart, but I liked it. Little was I to know that in the coming weeks I'd be trying nearly a hundred different types of hot tea. Basil had everything. He was particularly fond of English Breakfast and Peppermint, however, so those varieties showed up more often than any others. On my first day on the job I didn't know all that was coming, but I enjoyed the Black Currant immensely.

Just after my first sip, the little dogs I'd met the day before pounced on me. Taylor and Devon were every bit as excited to see me as they had been the day before and my face was soon wet with doggie kisses. They calmed down more quickly this time and I was able to sit and talk with Basil more or less undisturbed.

He engaged me in idle chitchat, asking me about my hobbies and what I was studying and so forth. While we talked I looked about me. We were sitting at an oak kitchen table that had lion paws for feet. It looked like it was over a hundred years old. Basil's home was quite peculiar. It wasn't divided into a lot of different rooms like most houses, but was just one big room. Only the bathroom and another small room were separate. I liked it. It was open and airy.

As my eye roved around the room I saw many things that looked just as old, or older, than the table. There were also all kinds of herbs hanging on the walls and from the ceiling, big bunches of them, some freshly cut and some quite dried out. They gave the atmosphere an earthy, but not unpleasant smell. In fact, the scent of the room somewhat reminded me of the potpourri that my mother purchased. But I don't think that Basil had them there for the scent. There was a pot bubbling away on the old gas stove that gave off the strongest odor of all. I was tempted to ask what it was, but I didn't want to appear too nosy on my very first day.

The whole room awakened my curiosity; it was unlike any I'd ever seen in my life. Some things there were quite ordinary, like the refrigerator, but other things were quite odd. The stove itself was gas, but looked like a wood burning stove I'd seen in the county historical museum on a field trip. Instead of built-in cabinets, there was a huge cupboard and some kind of antique kitchen cabinet with a white metal work surface. There was also a large wooden trunk that bore a slight resemblance to a coffin, and a lot of ancient furniture. Basil's home looked quite new on the outside, but quite old on the inside. I felt as if I'd walked into another world.

As I talked, Basil seemed completely unimpressed with some of the subjects I mentioned. He didn't say so, but I had the distinct impression that he thought some of my classes a complete waste of time. I'd never come across an adult with that kind of attitude before. I was quickly learning, however, that Basil was anything but a typical adult. He seemed more like an immensely wise and intelligent child.

We talked until we'd finished our tea, then Basil drew a short list out of his pocket.

"I need you to go to the apothecary and pick up some parcels for me," he said. "Tell him to put them on my account."

"Um, uh…a-pot-o-carry?" I had no clue as to what he meant.

"The pharmacist, the man who handles medicines at the drug store."

"Oh! I get it." I was fast learning that not only did Basil speak in a particular manner, he seemed to have his own words for some things. I concentrated very hard to remember that apothecary meant pharmacist.

"When you pick up the parcels, give him this list and ask him to see if he can find what is on it. Got that?"

"Yes."

"Off you go then, Graham. I'll see you when you return."

I stepped out the door and strolled down the lane. It was a couple of miles into town, but I didn't mind. I liked walking and I was even getting paid! Once in town, it wouldn't take me long to reach the drug store. Our town was small and there was nothing that was very distant. As I walked into town I pulled the list from my pocket and read it:

Angelica 1 oz.
Hyssop 2 ozs.
Camphor 1 oz.
Myrrh 3 ozs.
Sandalwood 1 oz.
Benzoin 1 oz.

I wondered if the drug store would have any of that stuff or could even get it. It seemed a very odd list to me. I'd never even heard of any of those things. I supposed they were more herbs like Basil had in his kitchen, but I wasn't even sure of that.

When I handed the pharmacist, or apothecary, the list, he didn't seem in the least bit fazed. Apparently it was not unusual to receive such a list from Basil. He read down it and frowned only slightly.

"Tell Mr. Diggory that I can have most of this for him in a couple of days. It might take a bit longer for the Myrrh, however." He looked up at me. "I take it you are the boy he told me about, the one who will be running errands for him?"

"Yes, that's me," I said proudly.

The apothecary smiled.

"Do you have any parcels for him?" I asked, using Basil's term "parcels" instead of packages, as I'd normally have done.

"Oh yes, here you go," said the apothecary pulling out two small parcels from beneath the counter wrapped in plain brown paper. I wondered what was in them.

"Mr. Diggory said to add them to his account."

With that I was on my way. I was eager to return to Basil's house. It was quite an interesting place. I'd only begun to look around the inside, but what I'd seen so far was fascinating. One thing I noticed about the house is that it was much roomier than it looked. I knew it was ridiculous, but I almost felt as if it really were bigger on the inside that on the outside. It couldn't be, but it sure looked like it. Perhaps the fact that it was pretty much just one big room made it seem that way. Still, it seemed a fair size bigger than it looked from the outside.

In no time at all I was back. Basil took the packages from me and unwrapped them. There were dried herbs inside that looked much like the ones hanging from the walls and ceiling.

"Good, good, this is the one I've been needing," he said. "Now we'll see if this works." He emptied the entire contents of one of the packages into the pot that was simmering on the stove. There was a large poof of green smoke and a scent of something like brussel sprouts filled the room.

"Now that's quite a nasty smell," said Basil, wrinkling his nose. I readily agreed with him. "Another failure," he said, looking into the pot. He didn't seem terribly surprised or disappointed.

"Just what is that? If you don't mind me asking," I said.

"It's just a little project of mine," he said. "Something I've been trying to perfect for quite a long time. I can never seem to get it quite right, however. I still can't find quite the right ingredients." Basil was lost in thought for a few moments as if mentally running down a checklist. His answer didn't really tell me much, but as no further explanation seemed forthcoming, I left my curiosity unsatisfied. I didn't want to appear nosy and I was working for him. Still, I wondered just what project he was working on.

"Now then, I have another errand for you to run," he said, producing another list from his pocket. "I should have sent this along with you when you went to the apothecary for me, but I just wasn't thinking. I hope you don't mind all this walking."

"Oh, not at all," I said.

"Good, good." He smiled. "I'm sure you'll know where to go to fill the list. Just tell them to put it on my account. Now I have to get this mess cleaned up."

I set out for the second time that day on an errand for Basil. I rather liked my new job. I looked at the list as I was leaving the yard, wondering what oddities I would find upon it. It was quite unlike the other, however. It read:

    one dozen large eggs (brown)
    one pound of brown sugar
    one pound of powdered sugar
    half a gallon of milk
    one package of vanilla cream cookies
    one extra large chocolate bar

Now this list I understood. I walked toward the grocery, enjoying the fine sunny weather.

It was a fair walk to the grocery store. It was on the far side of town. There was but one and it was rather small. It was well stocked, however, and had just about anything one could want. I'd been there any number of times with my parents, although they usually went to the big supermarket in the next town. Basil seemed to like to get everything locally. I wondered why I'd never seem him around town before. The first time I set eyes on him was the day I answered his ad. Ours was a small town, one of those where everyone knows everyone else (and their business), but I couldn't recall ever having seen Basil. There seemed a great deal about him that was rather particular, although his grocery list was ordinary enough.

As I neared the grocery, my eyes were automatically drawn to the skyline. There, visible over the tops of the trees were the latticework supports of a towering roller coaster. There'd been a big amusement park a mile or so outside of town, but it had been closed for years—locked up tight. I'd been there a couple times, before it shut down. I didn't remember much about it because I was only five or six when it closed. I did have vague memories of cotton candy and laughing on a carousel. It really sucked that it wasn't still running, but there'd been some kind of accident on the big coaster, the one visible over the trees, and that was the end of the place. I didn't know much about it, but I'd heard people talking. It was kind of amazing that there'd ever been an amusement park so close to our little town. It seemed much too small of a place for it to be.

Some of the high school guys went there sometimes. There was supposed to be a hole in the fence somewhere right near the coaster on the edge of the park. I'd never been brave enough to sneak in. There was talk that the park was haunted by kids that had been killed in the accident. I don't even know if anyone was killed or not, but that was the story anyway. If there was an abandoned amusement park, where someone might have been killed, you could be sure there'd be ghost stories about it. I'm sure there was nothing to it, but there was still something eerie about the park.

The grocery store blocked my view of the coaster as I drew near. I entered and grabbed a cart. I found I rather liked grocery shopping. I'd never done it alone before. It took me a while to find some of the things on the list as I didn't know my way around very well. I had an especially hard time locating the extra large chocolate bar, as I was looking at the section by the checkout with all the normal sized candy bars. I was just wondering if Basil would mind if I substituted a couple of smaller bars for a larger one when I thought of looking in the section with the bags of candy. I found it quick enough when I looked there and was soon approaching the checkout.

I was a little apprehensive, as I'd never heard of anyone having an account with a grocery. Then again, I hadn't heard of anyone having one with a pharmacist either. When I told the checkout lady to put it on Mr. Diggory's account she didn't bat an eye.

I made my way back, weighted down with my purchases. The bag wasn't terribly heavy, but it did make my arms ache a bit carrying it for such a long distance. I frowned; I didn't like being reminded that I was less than muscular. My arms were very thin and my biceps small. Everything about me seemed small and I didn't like it at all. I didn't let it get me down. There was no use in that. It was a fine afternoon and I was getting paid for what I was doing to boot!

It wasn't long before I was back at Basil's. He was busily adding herbs in careful measure to the bubbling pot. I guess he'd dumped it and had started again on whatever it was he was making. He looked up and smiled when I entered.

"Just put those things away for me, will you, Graham?"

I stuck the eggs and milk in the refrigerator, and then began opening the doors of the big cupboard and the old fashioned kitchen cabinet trying to find out where everything went. Behind some of the doors were ordinary, everyday things, while behind others were little jars filled with all sorts of unusual herbs and other oddities—all labeled. I noticed one in particular marked "powdered goat intestine". It sounded disgusting to me.

Soon enough I'd found a place for everything, except the chocolate bar.

"Where should I put this?" I asked.

"Oh, the chocolate bar is for you," said Basil with a smile. "You do like chocolate, I hope."

"Oh yes," I said. "Very much, thank you!"

"Have a seat and have some then, while you tell me what you did today."

I sat at the table with lion's paw feet and told Basil what I thought he might find interesting about my day, although there wasn't much interesting to tell. As I did so, I swung my legs back and forth, nibbled on the enormous chocolate bar, and scratched Taylor and Devon behind the ears. As soon as I'd sat down they were right there wanting attention. Devon was pawing me for a share of my candy.

"Don't give him any chocolate," said Basil. "It's toxic for dogs you know."

"I've heard that," I said.

Basil walked over to the cabinet and gave each of the dogs a biscuit. That seemed to content them for a moment, although Devon was still eyeing my chocolate.

We talked for a good long while until it was time for me to go. I couldn't wait to come back and I hadn't even left yet. I couldn't believe I was getting paid so much for a job that I loved so well. I smiled all the way home.

CHAPTER 3

❦

The Twins and The Wolf

Every single day for the next week, I sat with Josiah at lunch. We didn't speak much, and what little conversation we had was awkward and halting. I would have given up completely, but I sensed that Josiah enjoyed my company, even though he didn't show it. Still, I was growing increasingly discouraged. I was getting a little depressed too. I was doing my best with Josiah, but he wasn't encouraging in the least. I was beginning to wonder if anyone at all wanted me. I wondered what was wrong with me. I couldn't even make a boy who was obviously lonely my friend.

Josiah was an odd one. In some ways, he seemed very confident and strong, but in others he was vulnerable. His eyes were almost mournful at times. His expression reminded me of the way I felt when I was sitting in the park watching other boys play basketball—wishing they'd ask me to join, but knowing they wouldn't. Josiah's expression was that of someone who was sitting on the sideline of life, not taking part in the joys of others. It was sad.

I wondered why Josiah wasn't more outgoing. He was the kind of boy who would've been asked to play basketball in the park. He was a good height and looked reasonably strong. He was probably an athlete and *those* guys *always* got asked to play. Josiah wasn't a little runt, like me, so it made his reluctance to get involved in things that much more confusing.

I all but gave up on the idea of Josiah as a boyfriend. I couldn't even get Josiah to show interest in being my friend, so it wasn't very likely he'd want an even more personal and intimate relationship. I wasn't sure about the whole idea myself. I didn't know if I could handle a boyfriend, or even if it's what I wanted. I was kind of confused about my feelings. I knew I was attracted to boys, but then again I was just thirteen. Maybe getting excited by guys like Josiah and Bry was just some kind of stage or something. I wished I had someone I could ask. I thought about calling Uncle Rob, but it was hard to talk about that kind of thing.

Despite the problems, I couldn't get Josiah out of my mind. I saw him often right after school, in the distance, walking alone. He traveled the very same route that I used, for a while at least, but then he'd turn off and disappear. I was very curious about Josiah, so I attempted to follow him one afternoon. I saw him leaving the school grounds as always, heading toward the western edge of town. I closed the distance between us a bit, but was careful not to get too close. I didn't want him thinking I was some crazed stalker. I laughed at that thought. I was too small and puny to be much of a threat to anyone. I was about as dangerous as a puppy or a baby bunny. I got a mental picture of a little bunny chasing kids around at school. *Look out! It's a killer bunny!* I laughed to myself. Sometimes, I was so odd.

I followed Josiah as he made the turn I saw him make everyday. He kept on for a good long while, until he turned again, heading for the very edge of town. I lost sight of him after he took the corner. When I reached the corner myself, he was gone. I was perplexed. He'd only turned the corner a few moments before, but he was nowhere to be seen. I didn't see how he'd have time to duck out of sight, even if he knew I was following him. I didn't think he was aware of my tailing him. I walked on down the street, but there was no sign of him at all. I guessed that I just wasn't very good at being a spy.

I thought to myself as I walked home. Maybe I was becoming a little obsessed with Josiah. Then again, maybe I spent so much time thinking about him because I had no one else to think about. Well, I had Bry to think about, but it wasn't like we'd *ever* become friends. I wasn't even sure he saw me when he looked at me. It was like I was invisible or something. Bry usually only talked to hot babes and cool dudes. I definitely wasn't cool.

Maybe I wasn't really obsessed with Josiah; perhaps I was merely intrigued. He was dark and mysterious. I just knew he was a fascinating guy. If only I could get him to loosen up a little and speak more than a few words at a time. I wanted to get closer to him, but he wasn't making it easy. It was like there was a wall around him or somethin'. I intended to climb over it, or get through it, or something. I just knew that Josiah and I could be close buds if he let me in.

The next day at lunch I carefully observed Josiah, but he showed no sign that he knew I'd been following him. Nothing had changed. Of course, lack of change wasn't a good thing. I was going nowhere fast. Or, as my grandpa would've put it: *I was doin' a lot of choppin', but no chips were flyin'.*

One thing *was* changing, though. More people were talking to me at school. At first it was just Kelly and her handful of friends, but several other girls had engaged me in conversation as well. The topic was always Josiah. He had captured their interest but wasn't any more forthcoming with conversation with the girls than he was with me; even less so apparently. They all saw me sitting with him everyday, so they considered me the best source for details about him. I didn't really have much to tell them, as Josiah rarely spoke more than a word or two at a time, but I still knew more than anyone else. I knew that all those girls wanted was information about their dream boy, but it was still nice that they were at least talking to me.

The girls weren't the only ones curious about Josiah. I was very surprised when Bry grabbed me by the arm and pulled me to the side in the hallway. I swallowed hard and looked at him fearfully. I figured I was in for it. I thought he was going to give me a rough time for some imagined slight. Or maybe he'd noticed me checking him out. I couldn't help myself. Whenever he was near, I just had to look at his muscles, and a few other things besides—like the way his tight jeans looked from the back—whew. I fought to keep my gaze from drifting while he spoke to me. I was afraid he'd deck me if he caught me looking at the bulge in his jeans, or his chest as it pushed out against his shirt.

I was stunned when he asked me about Josiah, and relieved as well. Bry wasn't going to pound me. He just wanted to know more about his rival. Josiah was getting a lot of attention and Bry didn't like it. I think what bothered him the most was Josiah's total lack of interest in all the attention he was receiving. He was getting it without trying, without wanting it, and it was driving Bry crazy.

"I'd stay away from him if I were you," said Bry after he'd pumped me for what little information I possessed.

"Why?" I asked.

"He's a freak. He barely talks to anyone. He keeps to himself. He isn't involved in anything; no sports, no clubs, nothing. A guy like that has something to hide. He's the kind that's all quiet and then one day comes in and kills everyone."

"I can't imagine Josiah doing anything like that," I told him.

"No one ever does, until it happens."

Bry left me standing there a bit frightened. I didn't really believe what he said about Josiah being dangerous, but Bry was right about one thing at least—Josiah was odd. He was unlike any boy I'd known, not that I knew any all that well. Still, there was something different about him.

I stiffened as I was digging books out of my locker. Jay, one of the twins, was opening his own locker not five feet away. Bry hadn't roughed me up as I'd feared, but I knew Jay would be only too happy to give me grief. He wasn't paying any attention to me, however, he was far too busy talking to the latest girl he was trying to charm. Apparently he'd succeeded with this one. I couldn't help but overhear them talking.

"Does it hurt much, Jay?"

"No, and please quit talking about it. I told you it's okay."

Kristi frowned at him and Jay quickly adjusted his attitude.

"It's sweet of you to worry, but it's nothing really." I wondered if girls really fell for his crap.

"You know you could get rabies or something. Dogs carry rabies sometimes you know."

Kristi pulled back the collar of Jay's shirt to get a better look. I couldn't help but look too. There were two puncture marks on Jay's lower neck, about two or three inches apart. Something had bit him. I couldn't think of anyone who deserved it more. I wish I knew what dog had done it, so I could give him a biscuit.

Jay caught me looking and quickly pulled his collar up.

"What are you looking at, runt?" he snarled, forgetting for the moment to be charming in front of Kristi.

I closed my locker and got out of there fast. I knew he probably wouldn't hurt me with that girl there, but I didn't want to give him any reason to come after me. He likely would anyway, but the more reason he had, the more he'd hurt me.

When I saw Jay a bit later in the day, he was looking daggers at me. You'd have thought I'd done something terrible to him. I knew I was in for it. I'd only seen him look like that once, just before he and his brother beat the crap out of me simply because I'd compared them to apes. I'd planned to follow Josiah after school once more, to see if

I could figure out where he lived, but I decided I'd better hurry home as quick as I could. I didn't want to give Jay a chance to ambush me. I knew he'd get me sooner or later, but later was better. The more time that passed, the more Jay would forget about whatever he was all worked up about. He was strong, but he wasn't awfully smart.

After school, I shoved the books I wouldn't need into my locker. I didn't want to be weighted down because I knew I'd probably have to run for it. I thought for a while about whether I should leave as soon as possible or wait around until Jay had gone home. I decided it would be best to get out of school as fast as I could. If I waited, Jay might come in looking for me and there'd be no witnesses, so he could do whatever he wanted to me.

I avoided the front entrance and slipped out a side door instead. I scurried along, even though there was no sign of Jay. I decide not to take my regular route. Instead I went the same way I did when I was following Josiah. My plan was to cut cross-country and come out near my home, avoiding the main road. Jay was most likely on the bus, but if he was waiting to ambush me, he'd probably do it on the road where we both lived. Riding the bus would get him home first too.

I reached the edge of town and headed out across country. There were a few open areas, but it was mostly woods. After a few, short minutes, I came across a long, winding drive. I had no idea I was so close to the old Maclaine house. If I'd had my wits about me, I'd have known my route would practically take me through the front yard. I couldn't see the house because of all the trees, but I knew it was there. I'd avoided it all my life. It was haunted and the stuff of legends. It had sat empty a long time, but rumor was some rich industrialist had bought it and was restoring it. I was in no mood to see it, and thought I'd better be moving along in any case, I'd heard rich people could get nasty if you trespassed on their land.

I heard a twig snap behind me and jerked my head around. My eyes opened wide in horror. It was Jay. His twin brother Clay was with him. They smiled evilly. I'd been so lost in my own thoughts I hadn't noticed them following me. They must have been, all the way from the school, because there was no reason for them to be hanging around the Maclaine place.

I bolted. Speed was my only chance for escape. Almost before I'd started, I tripped and went down hard. Jay and Clay grabbed me before I even had a chance to stand up. I was feeling extremely frightened, as well as amazingly stupid and uncoordinated.

"Well, well, if it isn't little Graham. Walking lessons not going so well I see," said Jay in a sickening sweet voice. "What are you doing out here? Ghost hunting?"

I didn't say a word. All I could think about was how they'd be hitting me in a moment. I wasn't fond of pain.

"Answer me, punk!" yelled Jay.

"I was avoiding you," I said. He smiled. He liked that he frightened me.

I knew it was time to pay for the little incident that morning. I hadn't really done anything of course, but Jay didn't need much of a reason to pick on me. I struggled against him and Clay, but they were like a million times stronger than me. I watched for my chance to escape. If they let go of me for even a second, I'd be out of there in a flash. The twins knew better than that, however. I'd escaped from them that way once too often.

I swallowed hard, wondering what they had planned for me. The twins could be quite ingenious in tormenting me. If they didn't simply beat me senseless, they'd do something nasty to me. They'd even tied me to an anthill once and smeared honey on me. Luckily, they had let me go just a few minutes later, but I still got bit by a lot of ants.

I'd never done anything to the twins, not even once, so I guess they liked picking on me because it was so easy. They were way bigger and stronger than I was. I didn't have a chance against them and that's just the way they liked it. I wanted to call them cowards, but I knew I'd get punched in the face for it.

They didn't usually hurt me too bad, just roughed me up a bit and called me names. I had walked away with a bloody nose or lip a few times, however. Sometimes they hurt me worse. It was never an enjoyable experience.

Jay hit me hard in the stomach and I doubled over while they laughed at me. I looked up at them with watery eyes. It hurt a lot. Jay could hit hard.

"Oh, you gonna be a little crybaby now, Graham?" said Jay. They laughed at me some more. I think their laughing hurt me more than the punch had, even though I shouldn't have let them get to me.

"Let's see if he's gonna cry," said Clay and took his turn punching me hard in the stomach.

The second punch hurt much worse than the first and I did start crying. I didn't make any sound, but water was streaming from my eyes. My stomach hurt bad enough I stayed hunched over. My mind wasn't really on the pain, however, it was on something I'd seen. Clay had two little marks on his neck just like Jay. I knew they always hung out together, but it was really odd that they had both been bit in the same place. I didn't have time to think about it much, the twins were far from finished with me.

"Come on, runt, it couldn't hurt that bad," said Jay "You're so small there's not much to hurt. I bet it wouldn't even hurt you if I kicked you where it counts. You don't have any…."

I was getting really upset. I just knew Jay was going to kick me in the balls next. I noticed, however, that he'd suddenly stopped talking. I wiped my eyes and looked around. Josiah was standing not far behind me, off to one side.

"What are you looking at, freak?" Jay said to him.

Josiah gave Jay a look of total contempt.

"I'm looking at two cowards who are so pathetic they get their kicks from picking on someone half their size."

I felt like warning Josiah to hold his tongue. He was bigger than me, but he was quite a bit smaller than either of the twins. He was going to get his ass kicked if he kept going. It was probably too late already.

As much as it terrified me, I determined that I'd do whatever I could to help him if they jumped him, which they undoubtedly would. He'd come to my aid, so the least I could do was get my butt kicked with him.

"You've got a smart mouth, you little British queer," said Clay. As he said it, both he and Jay lunged for Josiah. I saw Jay aim a hard punch right at Josiah's nose. Josiah blocked it in midair and punched Jay so hard in the stomach that Jay just fell to the ground clutching himself. His mouth gaped open and there was this sound coming from it like he was trying desperately to breathe, but was unable to do so. Clay flung himself at Josiah. I raced to help him, but Josiah grabbed Clay by the front of his shirt and tossed him away like a rag doll. My eyes grew wide and I gasped as Clay went flying. He hit the ground hard and looked totally dazed. I didn't blame him.

I just stood there gaping at Josiah. He wasn't even breathing hard. Jay and Clay were staring at him. Jay was still clutching his stomach and Clay was lying there shocked.

The twins weren't ready to give up yet. They were two of the toughest boys in school. They both dove for Josiah at the same time. Josiah grabbed Jay by the front of his shirt and Clay by the arm. He sent them sailing through the air to land more than ten feet from him. I simply could not believe my eyes. The twins couldn't believe what had just happened either. They just sat there looking up at Josiah in terror.

"Beat it," said Josiah.

I'll never forget seeing the twins run for it. I don't think even I could have run that fast. They were scared witless. Josiah stood there looking at them as they departed, not a hair out of place.

"You okay, Graham?" he asked me. He sounded so calm and collected, as if nothing at all had happened. His British accent made him sound so civilized.

"Yeah, thanks," I said.

I wanted to ask Josiah how he'd gotten so strong, but he turned on his heel and was gone in an instant. I didn't even have a chance to thank him properly. I just stood there for a few moments, stunned. I'd never seen anyone take on the twins before and I'd sure never seen any boy toss two guys that probably weighed a hundred and fifty pounds each ten feet away without working up a sweat. Josiah didn't even look all that muscular. How could he possibly be that strong?

I didn't have time to ponder Josiah as I needed to hurry on to Basil's. I didn't want to be late for work and I knew it would take me some time to get there going through the woods. I had a feeling I had no need to worry about the twins for a few days at least.

I rushed along to the little house up the lane, running part of the way. Basil looked up and smiled at me when I opened the door and his two little dogs jumped around me in circles and pawed at me. I scratched them behind the ears and petted them and they scampered away to play with one of the many stuffed toys that were strewn about the floor.

"Sit down my boy and have a cup of tea. Raspberry this time."

I smiled and sat across from Basil. Every time I'd been to his house, he'd offered me a different kind of tea. I wondered just how many varieties he had. I found that I liked the raspberry quite a lot. It had a sweet, fruity taste that was quite enjoyable. It even made my stomach feel better. It was still aching from being punched.

"An excellent job on the garden, Graham, and the geraniums have never looked better." Basil's eyes sparkled whenever he spoke. He had a way of making me feel very good about everything I did. I'd only weeded the garden and watered the geraniums the evening before, but he made it sound like I'd been tending them for weeks.

"I had a little trouble with the garden," I said. "I didn't know if some of the plants were herbs or weeds, so I was afraid to pull them."

"You are a wise lad. That's why I chose you. The moment I set eyes on you, I knew you were just the boy for the job. Tell you what, I'll teach you a bit about herbs so you'll know how to tell them apart from the weeds."

We sat and talked while we finished our tea. I told Basil about my weekend, and my day at school. I didn't tell him everything of course, but I told him quite a lot. When we were done, Basil led me outside to his little garden.

"Why don't you tell me which ones you recognize first and we can go from there," he said.

I pointed out some oregano and peppermint, and some parsley and sage. That was about as far as I could get.

"Very good. I'm surprised you know even that much. Most boys don't seem to go in for herb lore this days, but it is interesting stuff!"

He began pointing out plants.

"This one here, the tall one with the purple flowers, is called Hyssop. It's used to heal wounds and bruises. This wrinkled fellow here is called horehound and is good for curing sore throats. This short plant with the pink flower is a weed." Basil pulled out the offending plant and tossed it away.

I was very glad I hadn't pulled out any plants I couldn't recognize as many that I thought were just weeds were indeed herbs and many that I thought were herbs or flowers were just weeds. Basil went on for quite a long time. I'd never thought herbs very interesting, but I had no idea how many things one could do with them.

"This pretty little guy here," said Basil pointing to a dark green plant with shiny leaves, "is called Sweet Alexander's Death. It tastes absolutely wonderful I've read, like watermelon candy."

"Why have you never tried it?" I asked.

"Because it's deadly poisonous. One bite and you're gone like that," he said, snapping his fingers. "The most important thing to remember is to never, ever taste a plant you don't know about and can't identify with absolute certainty. Many are quite harmless, but others are quite deadly, and it's often the most harmless looking plants that are the most lethal. See that tiny plant there, with the bright yellow flower at the top?"

I nodded my head.

"If you so much as put that one in your mouth it will give you such stomach pains you'll feel like your insides are being roasted. It won't kill you, but it will make you wish you were dead."

"Why do you keep such dangerous plants in your garden?" I asked.

"They all have uses, my boy. Practically everything in life is dangerous, if used improperly. That gold chain around your neck, for instance. Take it and run it across your skin quickly and it will cut like a saw. Pull up on it hard enough and it will choke you. Don't do those things and it's perfectly safe. It's the same with these plants. Taste "Sweet Alexander's Death" and it will kill you instantly, but simmer it with Roseroot and Yarrow for an hour and it will heal most any wound, no matter how serious."

"What's this one here?" I asked, pointing out the lemony smelling one I'd noticed on Saturday.

"Ah, that one is called Lemon Balm. It will sooth insect bites and sores, relieve headaches and tension. It also wards off vampires and makes a rather good tea."

I looked quickly at Basil as he mentioned vampires, but he appeared not to notice. I half expected to find him smiling as if he were pulling my leg, but he seemed quite serious. I opened my mouth to ask him if he was kidding, but I thought better of it.

My herb lesson continued for a few minutes more and then we went back inside. Basil set me to dusting the many bottles that he kept in shelves about the kitchen area. Most of them were labeled with words I couldn't understand, Latin I supposed, but many of the words seemed even more bizarre. Even dusting was interesting work at Basil's house.

❧   ❧   ❧

Late that night I awoke from a rather pleasant dream, which I could not remember. I wondered why I'd awakened, or more precisely, what had awakened me. I turned my eyes to the window and for just a moment I could have sworn I saw someone there, or something. It was more like a shadow among the shadows than anything else and its mere presence filled me with dread. I forced myself to slide out of bed and walk toward the window.

As I looked out into the yard I could see bright eyes intently peering at me. The eyes were gone in an instant and then I saw the form of a great dog slipping into the shadows. I knew it was no dog, however; it was the wolf I'd seen some days before, unless of course there was more than one of them. I was very disturbed that it had been looking at me. I was very disturbed that it was there at all. Why was it there? How did it know where I lived?

I shook my head to clear it. I was thinking nonsense. Wolves did not track people down. They might follow their scent, but they certainly didn't go about looking up addresses in phone books to stalk their victims. Maybe the wolf had followed my scent home a few nights before. That seemed to make a bit of sense. It still made me feel uneasy. A wolf was stalking me when there shouldn't even be any wolves around, except in zoos.

Perhaps someone had one as a pet and it ran away, I thought to myself. I had heard of people having wolf/husky mixes. Perhaps that's what I'd seen. I didn't really know what a wolf looked like after all. It could well have been part wolf and part dog. That made me feel a bit better, but it still didn't explain why it had been peering at me through my window. The dark shadow just outside made me believe that it had been right up against my window looking in. It was all very peculiar.

My heart pounded in my chest as a thought occurred to me. Both the twins had been bitten by something, probably some kind of dog, perhaps even a wolf. The thought made me more uncomfortable than ever. I felt almost as if a serial killer were on the loose and I was the next victim.

I went back to bed, but did not sleep easily. When I did manage to nod off, I had dreams about wolves chasing me through the woods. I tried to get back to my pleasant dream, the one I couldn't quite remember, but I couldn't find my way back. Why was it that I could never dream what I wanted?

CHAPTER 4

The Ice Thaws at Last

Before lunch the next day, a small, but rather significant thing happened. Josiah Huntington actually said "hello" to me in the hall. I hadn't even said "hi" to him first. He just said "hello" as he passed and then hurried on, but it was the first time he'd ever initiated any type of contact with me, or with anyone else for that matter.

When I came and sat by Josiah at lunch, he actually smiled slightly when he looked up and noticed me. His smile was barely perceptible, but it was there. Anyone else would have missed it, but I knew him better than any living soul. What's more, he actually said, "Hello, Graham." He had greeted me twice in one day. He'd even remembered my name.

"Those guys give you any more trouble?" he asked.

"Not yet," I said, "and they probably won't for a while. You really scared them."

"Yeah, I probably went a little far. I didn't mean to, but it makes me so angry when I see guys picking on someone like that."

I couldn't believe Josiah was actually speaking to me. He'd never uttered such a long string of words before.

"Well, I appreciate what you did and I don't think you went too far at all. If you hadn't come along they'd have beat me senseless. I'd have tried to fight them off, but they are far too big for me."

I nearly pointed out that they were far too big for Josiah too, but that almost sounded rude, so I took another tact.

"Um, how is it that you were able to toss Jay and Clay like that? I mean, they've got to weigh a hundred and fifty pounds or so each and you just tossed them like they weighed nothing."

Josiah looked a bit frightened for a moment, but then coolly answered me.

"It's all a matter of momentum and leverage. They were running at me, so I used their own power and speed against them. I've had a few lessons in self defense."

That didn't quite seem to explain it to me. For one thing, Josiah had thrown them back the way they came. If he'd used their own momentum to throw them like he claimed, wouldn't he have had to throw them in the direction they were already going, instead of the opposite one? It looked to me like he'd stopped their momentum entirely and had lifted them and tossed them, one with each arm. Maybe I hadn't seen what I thought I did, however. It all happened so fast. I looked at Josiah. He seemed pretty solidly built, but he was slim and compact, not muscular. He couldn't have lifted those boys and tossed them like I thought he did. If he was strong enough to do that he'd have had muscles bulging out all over.

"Man, this Salisbury steak is really bad," said Josiah, wrinkling his nose. His British accent made everything he said sound so suave.

"Welcome to the Griswold Jr.-Sr. High Cafeteria," I laughed. "It has a negative five star rating you know."

Josiah smiled at me. He was especially attractive when he smiled. I noticed a few girls watching him. I'm sure they wouldn't fail to notice how a smile improved his looks. Josiah took no notice of them, however. He just idly poked at his lima beans.

"You sure negative five stars is enough?" Josiah was beginning to act like a real boy at last. I'm not quite sure what had done it, but his icy attitude was beginning to melt away. I was glad I'd kept talking to him and sitting with him even though he'd acted like he didn't want me around.

"You wanna hang out after school sometime?" I asked. "I have to work most of the time, but I have Fridays off, or we could do something on the weekend sometime. You know, watch a movie, or get pizza…or something."

I was speaking a little quickly. What I was asking was much more important to me that Josiah could possibly realize. If he said "yes" it would be a major step to us becoming friends, and maybe even more. I felt like we were friends already, since he'd saved my butt, but I knew he might not see it that way at all. I desperately wanted a friend, and I just knew Josiah would be an especially cool one.

Josiah didn't answer right away, instead he took a bite of the questionable Salisbury steak and chewed slowly. I could tell he was giving my invitation a lot more thought than it really required. He looked just a touch sad.

"Yeah," he said at last. "Yeah. That sounds like fun."

"Great!" I said, smiling from ear to ear. The day was getting better and better.

Josiah smiled back at me for a moment. He remained pretty quiet for the rest of lunch. He seemed a bit awkward and ill at ease speaking with me. He seemed to have a great deal on his mind, although I couldn't imagine what it must be. I didn't mind that he was quiet. I was used to it and felt closer to having him as a friend than ever before.

That afternoon I made yet another attempt to find out where Josiah lived, but I did it in an entirely different way. I supposed that he must have been on the way home when he discovered the twins working me over. Instead of tailing him as I had before, I left school as fast as possible to get in front of him, and took the most direct route possible to the road near the old Maclaine place. Once there, I hid myself in the bushes and waited to see if Josiah would pass.

I waited and waited, but there was no sign of him. It wasn't a total waste of time, however. There were some very beautiful purple flowers nearby and a great many birds. I hadn't noticed the flowers the day before. Then again, I was far too busy getting pounded to take note of much of anything.

I'd almost forgotten what I was doing there when I heard someone approach. I peered through the bushes to see Josiah walking up the road. He turned off onto the lane that led to the old Maclaine place. I crept from my hiding place and followed. I was ever so careful because Josiah had a real knack for disappearing.

I hadn't trailed him long when the old Maclaine home loomed in the near distance. The trees kept it hidden until the lane took a bit of a turn and then there it was. It was a mansion really, three stories high, massive, and frightening. I'd heard it was being restored, but it looked untouched. I watched as Josiah walked up the stairs and disappeared inside. *So that's where he lives*, I said to myself. Josiah must have been the son of the wealthy industrialist I'd heard had bought the place. That gave me cause for worry. If Josiah was a rich boy, he might not want anything to do with me. I kicked myself for being foolish. He'd never acted as if I wasn't good enough for him, not once. I looked at the house for a few moments longer, then crept away. I didn't want Josiah to see me spying on him.

🍁   🍁   🍁

I had a good feeling about Josiah. Things had changed with him. He was suddenly talking to me and even agreed to go out with me. It looked like we might actually become friends after all. I was so happy I felt like I could walk on air. It stirred up some other feelings inside me, however, feelings that confused me.

I liked Josiah. I liked him a lot. Thinking about him made me smile. It also gave me a feeling that is hard to describe; kind of cheerful and warm inside. Thoughts of holding his hand and walking alone together in the moonlight entered my mind. That made me feel good too, but I wasn't quite sure what I was feeling. The emotions that Josiah stirred up weren't the same as those created by Bry. I reacted to Bry physically, but Josiah made me *feel* things. Josiah was cute, and sexy, but I didn't really think of him like I thought about Bry. I didn't fantasize about him. It made me wonder if what I wanted from him was just friendship, or something more. Was I gay or straight? Just when I thought I knew pretty well for sure, I got all confused again.

I needed help and I could think of only one person who might be able to give me some guidance. I didn't feel comfortable talking to my parents about what I was feeling. I didn't feel like I could talk to Basil about certain things either. I definitely couldn't talk to Josiah because he was causing most of my confusion. The only person who I thought I might be able to talk to was Uncle Rob.

Admitting to anyone that I might be gay, or even that I was confused about my sexual orientation, was a major ordeal. Being gay was something no boy wanted to happen to him. Most boys acted like finding out you were gay was like finding out you had cancer or something. I didn't really feel that way myself, but I wasn't comfortable with the thought that I might be queer. I was enough of an outcast because I was small. I didn't really need to become even more of an outcast.

I waited until everyone was out of the house before I called Uncle Rob. I picked up the phone and put it back down three times before I could make myself dial his number. I made myself do it. I needed help and waiting would only make it worse. Uncle Rob's voice was cheerful when he answered. That put me at ease a bit. Uncle Rob had always liked me a lot.

As Uncle Rob and I started chatting, I began to feel a little better about the fact that I might be gay. Uncle Rob was cool. It had been quite a while since I'd visited him, but I remembered he had a nice house and a kick-ass car. He played football with his friends and was always going out and doing something fun. He took me to amusement parks whenever I went out to see him. He took me camping, too, and hiking. We did all kinds of stuff together. I'd never guessed that he was gay. Even since I'd learned it, I didn't think of him as gay. I just thought of him as Uncle Rob, the coolest guy I knew.

"Um, Uncle Rob?" I said, when we'd been talking quite a while, "Could I talk to you about something?" My stomach churned. I'd been talking about anything and everything, except what I'd called about. I didn't know where to start, or what to say.

"Of course you can, Graham. You can talk to me about anything, you know that."

"Well, um, did Mom tell you she told me about you?"

"About me?"

"Yeah, about you being, um…gay."

"No, she didn't tell me, but it's cool. Is that what you want to talk to me about?"

"Well, uh, kind of…really about me, though."

I felt a little frightened at that moment. It was so difficult talking about something I'd never talked about before.

"Graham, you know I love you. Nothing will change that. You're my favorite nephew after all."

"I'm your *only* nephew," I said smiling. It was kind of a running joke between us. Uncle Rob was always telling me I was his favorite nephew. Hearing it again now helped put me more at ease, as did him telling me he'd love me no matter what. I pretty much knew that without being told, but I needed to hear it just then.

"There's this boy at school. You know I don't really have any friends, any guy friends that is. Well anyway, there's this boy named Josiah. I've been talking to him and stuff. I eat lunch with him. We're going to go out and do something together soon, just have fun…you know. I'm kind of confused about him, or I guess about me."

"In what way?"

"Well, I really, really want him as a friend and I'm all happy because I think maybe he's going to be my friend. It's great when we have lunch together and stuff. But then there are these other feelings I have for him. Sometimes…sometimes I think I'd like to hold his hand, maybe even kiss him."

I swallowed hard. I had barely even admitted to myself that I wanted to kiss Josiah and here I was telling Uncle Rob about it.

"I don't know if I'm all excited over him because we might be friends, or if there's something more there, you know? I mean, I've never done anything with a girl. I don't even think I want to, and I'm having these feelings about Josiah. And then, there's this other guy, Bry…"

"What about him?"

"Well, we aren't friends. I don't think about holding his hand, but I think about other stuff. He's real good looking, tall, and built. I, um…"

I couldn't keep going. I couldn't tell my uncle that Bry's body gave me an erection.

"There was a guy I knew in high school," said Uncle Rob, "the boy you are talking about, the built one, sounds a lot like him. I used to kind of follow him around. He was gorgeous. He had muscles everywhere. I thought about him a lot. I had fantasies about him. I masturbated thinking about him."

Uncle Rob and I had never discussed such things before and I was nervous. It was helping, though.

"I, um, I think about Bry a lot too. I keep imagining us wrestling, and he has his shirt off, and it makes me…hard. I just…I'm so confused."

"It's okay, Graham. It's okay to be confused. Things like this aren't easy."

"I kind of think I might be gay, but I'm not sure. I mean, I've never done anything with anyone. I've got all these feelings inside me and sometimes I just feel like I'm gonna explode. Josiah is so great, but I don't know if I want him as a friend, or a boyfriend, or whatever. I don't think about girls the way I do Josiah and Bry, but it's not like I don't like them. I've heard all this stuff about boys my age experimenting and going through stages and stuff. I can't decide what I am. I mean—am I straight, or gay, or bi? It's just all too much."

"Graham, adolescence is a difficult time. Everything is changing and so much is expected of you. You aren't a little boy anymore, but you aren't yet a man either. Things can get really confusing, and frustrating. I don't think you need to worry about it so much. Don't try to label yourself. No matter what you do, you are going to be what you are going to be. Maybe this attraction you are feeling for other boys is a passing thing, or maybe you'll discover that you are gay. Maybe what you feel for Josiah is a strong feeling of friendship, or maybe you're beginning to fall in love. Only time will tell you about these things. I know it's confusing, but I suggest you just sit back and let nature take its course. It will all work out just as it's meant to work out, whether you worry about it or not. I know I can't tell you to just forget about it, but don't worry about it so much, okay? It sounds to me like you can have a good relationship with this Josiah, whether it's as a friend, or more. And Bry, well, he's the type of boy other boys admire. Maybe you have a bit of hero worship for him, or maybe a bit of lust. Either way, it's okay. Your parents are going to love you, no matter what happens, as will I."

"Are you sure? About my parents?"

"Listen, I know your mom. She found out I was gay when she was seventeen and I was fifteen. You know what she did when she found out?"

"No."

"She hugged me. She told me she loved me and she didn't care whether I liked boys or girls. She loves you, Graham, and that's not ever going to change. I'm sure it's the same with your dad."

"A lot of parents get mad when they find out their son is gay. They don't love them anymore. They make them go away." The very thought upset me. If I thought about it too long, I'd probably cry.

"Yes, that's true. It's sad and wrong, but it's true. Those are *other* parents though, Graham, not yours. Your parents will love you no matter what."

I wish there was some way I could hug Uncle Rob over the phone. I had tears in my eyes.

"I love you," I told him.

"I love you too, Graham, and I'll tell you something. I think of you as my son."

Wow! That hit me hard, in a good way. It felt good to have someone care about me that much. It felt good to have someone who understood, too.

"Well…uh…I don't know what else to say, so I guess I'd better get off here."

"Okay, Graham. You come and visit me when you get the chance, okay?"

"I sure will, Uncle Rob."

"And call me if you want to talk—about anything. I'll always be here for you, Graham."

"Thanks. Bye, Uncle Rob."

"Bye."

🍁   🍁   🍁

I walked to my special place in the woods after I'd talked with Uncle Rob. He made me feel a lot better about everything. He was probably right too. I probably didn't need to worry so much over whether I was gay or straight or whatever. I did want to know the answer, but it would come. Uncle Rob said I just needed to relax and see what happened. I decided to do that as much as I could. I knew I wouldn't be able to stop thinking or worrying about it, but maybe I could keep myself from getting so worked up over it. I couldn't change anything anyway. Whatever was going to happen, would happen. It sure made me feel a lot better knowing that my family would love me no matter what. It kind of made my sexual orientation unimportant. I was so glad I'd talked with Uncle Rob.

I wasn't so sure about my dad, though. I didn't think he'd kick me out of the house or anything, but I wasn't sure how he'd react if I found out I was gay. He didn't like Uncle Rob very much and I was pretty sure it was because he was gay. Uncle Rob seemed pretty sure of himself, but I thought he was being overly optimistic. I wasn't going to breathe a word about being gay to Dad until I was sure. I wasn't certain I'd tell him even then.

CHAPTER 5

❀

My First "Date"

My step was even lighter than usual as I walked to Basil's house, because I was thinking about the next evening. It had been nearly two weeks since I'd asked Josiah to do something with me, but at last it was about to happen. Josiah and I hadn't made any specific plans, but he was coming home with me after school. I didn't really care what we did. I was so excited to be spending time with him I knew I'd have fun no matter what. I really think I could have enjoyed an evening of watching paint dry if Josiah was by my side. Perhaps I was kind of pathetic for getting so excited over the simple idea of having a friend, but I didn't care. I bet Kelly would be plenty excited when I told her about it too, but for her own reasons. She might be a bit upset when she found out I hadn't invited her over, but I wanted some time alone with Josiah before I started including her. Besides, she'd probably just sit there and moon over him or something. There was also the little matter of my unresolved feelings for Josiah. I needed time to see where things were going.

I stepped onto Basil's little yard. The grass was neatly trimmed and the flowerbeds had not a weed in them. I'd been doing a really good job with the yard work. I was even getting a bit of a tan from it.

I walked inside and was greeted by Taylor and Devon, who jumped up on me and tried to lick my face. Basil was at the pot on the stove, carefully adding ingredients and stirring.

"Pour us some tea will you?" he asked. "It's all ready in the pot. Honey and Lemon, I'm sure you'll like it."

Basil kept on adding ingredients and stirring while I got out two blue and white cups and saucers and sat them on the kitchen table. I got the little aluminum teapot in which he brewed our tea and poured out two steaming cups. I caught the scent of the honey and lemon as the steam wafted gently into the air.

Basil was intent upon his simmering pot. I was always curious about it, but afraid to ask. Not once had I walked into Basil's little house without finding a pot simmering away on the stove. It was almost as if it just sat there continually bubbling away. I knew, however, that this was not the case. Often the contents were a dark, murky brown, but at other times they'd been greenish blue, nearly yellow, and even a creamy lavender. I caught a glimpse as I was putting the teapot back and noted that today the contents were a chunky cream color, with just the slightest tint of yellow. For the first time ever I screwed up my courage to ask Basil just what was in his pot.

"Our supper!" he announced immediately. "I do hope you are fond of potato soup! I was out in the garden earlier and dug up a few new potatoes and just couldn't keep myself from making some soup. Get some bowls out of the cupboard will you?"

I'd received a quick answer, but it seemed I'd asked at just the wrong time. I was certain that what was usually simmering in that pot was not some kind of soup. Now that I looked closer at it, I noted that it wasn't the same pot at all. It was quite similar, but definitely not the same one. I was relieved. I wasn't so sure I wanted to eat anything cooked in that other pot. Who knew what had been in it? I remembered only too well the jar marked "powdered goat intestine" that I'd seen in the cupboard.

I had not learned anything new about Basil, but the soup was delicious. I was wondering a great deal about him. He was unlike anyone I'd ever met before. He was very open and friendly, and yet he had an air of mystery and wonder about him. He seemed quite out of place in my little community. I lived near what was perhaps the most boring town on earth and Basil seemed far too interesting a person to be there.

For the moment, I just enjoyed my soup and the most wonderful job I'd ever had in my life. Okay, so it was about the only real job I'd ever had, but it sure beat the few other options that were open to me. It was way better than mowing lawns or having a paper route. I'd done both of those and didn't care much for them. I think I would have worked for Basil for free. If I was willing to do work for free then it was something I really enjoyed!

That afternoon I was running back and forth between Basil's little house, the post office, and the apothecary. There were so many packages and boxes that I couldn't carry them all at once. I wondered what was in them all. I was sure some of them were ingredients for Basil's pot, but some were far too heavy. A few of those that were heavy felt like they were probably books. Others I couldn't guess about at all. By the time I was done running errands it was time for me to go. I wanted to hang around a bit and see what was in various parcels and boxes, but I had a ton of homework and wanted to make sure I had everything cleared out of the way so I'd be completely free to spend all my time with Josiah the next afternoon.

🍁 🍁 🍁

I was a bit nervous all day at school, which was pretty silly. I'd had lunch with Josiah every single day for a few weeks, so it wasn't like he was a complete stranger. On the other hand, I didn't really feel like I knew all that much about him. We talked, but he never really told me anything about himself. I had no idea what he did for fun, what he was interested in, or even what sports he liked. He was still a stranger in many ways.

We met at my locker at the end of school. I was even more nervous than I had been all day. I stood there shifting my weight from one foot to the other, not knowing quite how to act.

Josiah seemed ill at ease himself, but he wasn't nervous. He just seemed a bit fearful. I grinned to myself. I couldn't remember anyone ever being afraid of me.

"Want to get a milkshake or something?" I asked. My stomach was growling a little and I thought it might make things easier if we could sit and eat something. After all, that's what we were used to doing.

"Sure," said Josiah smiling, "I haven't had ice cream in ages."

We walked out of the school and down the sidewalk. Josiah looked as if he felt a bit odd. Perhaps he was experiencing some of the same feelings I was. After all, he didn't have any real friends, at least none I'd ever seen. He was just as alone as me, even more so, since I had Kelly.

I caught a look of yearning in Josiah's eyes that gave me hope. It was a yearning for companionship and friendship. I was very glad to see it. Josiah had been very reluctant to do anything with me outside of school, but now that we were doing it at last he seemed very pleased.

It didn't take us long at all to get to Clarks. It was a little burger and ice cream place on Main Street. Clarks was decorated with a lot of rock and roll memorabilia. There were a lot of old concert posters hanging on the walls. I really liked the place for the food, however. It had great burgers and the best ice cream in town. I ordered a snicker twister, which is a big cup of ice cream with bits of caramel, chocolate, and nuts all mixed up in it. Josiah had never had one before, so he ordered the same.

I looked around for a table. The place was pretty much empty. I headed for a table in front of a big mirror, but Josiah grabbed my arm.

"Could we sit there instead," he said. "I want to watch while they make our twisters."

"Uh, sure," I said and we sat at a booth under a huge *Phantom* poster. I didn't care where we sat as long as I was with Josiah. I was thoroughly enjoying his company.

We sat in silence for a while. I finally worked up the courage to ask him one of the many questions that had been on my tongue for so long.

"Did you ever live in England, Josiah? You have a bit of an British accent."

"Yes, I lived there quite some time ago. I was born there in fact. My parents were both British."

"Cool," I said. "I love listening to you speak. I always thought you must have lived in England."

Josiah smiled shyly.

"How long have you been living in the U.S.?" I asked.

"For years," said Josiah. "I really think of this place as my home. It's been so long since I lived in England that it's hard to remember it sometimes."

"Yeah, I have trouble remembering things from when I was really little too."

Our twisters arrived and we dove in. I loved twisters, they were so creamy and sweet.

"This is heavenly," said Josiah smiling. He spooned out big globs of the chocolaty ice cream and devoured it. He went at it so voraciously that some of it dribbled down his chin. He laughed with a mouth full of ice cream as he reached for a napkin. I laughed, too.

We were really loosening up around each other. I wasn't nervous at all sitting there with Josiah. We ate ice cream, laughed, and joked around. At last I felt like I had a real friend. One I could talk to about guy stuff.

Some girls came in and played *Do You Know That I Love You* on the jukebox.

"I think it's like the millionth time I'd heard that song," I laughed. "Kelly loves it. She plays it over and over and over on her CD player and makes me listen to it every time it's on the radio, too."

"I don't think I've heard it before," said Josiah.

"You're kidding, right?" I said.

"No," he said, looking at me as if he didn't understand my astonishment.

"Oh, man, I thought everyone had heard it. It's on the radio all the time."

"I don't listen to the radio a lot," said Josiah, almost apologetically.

"No problem there," I said. "Kelly makes me listen all the time, especially if any *Phantom* songs are on. She has a huge crush on Jordan." I could tell Josiah had no idea who that was. He was really odd in some ways. Jordan was like the most famous boy in the whole freaking world and Josiah had never heard of him.

"She has a crush on you too," I said, casually.

"Oh?"

"But don't *ever* tell her I told you that. She'd kill me."

"I won't." He smiled.

After a while we took what was left of our ice cream and walked across the street to the park. We crossed the narrow area of grass and sat on its edge looking out over the little lake. It was a beautiful sight with the sun shimmering on the water.

The twins passed near to us, but didn't give us any trouble. I saw them eyeing Josiah. No doubt they were still remembering how he'd fought them off on that day they were picking on me. I was glad I was with Josiah. If he hadn't been there they'd have been on me for sure.

We finished our ice cream and then headed for my house. It was a beautiful Friday afternoon and neither of us minded the long walk into the country. I kept smiling. It just felt so good to have Josiah walking by my side. Being with him gave me a warm feeling in my chest. I was happy. Things were going really well. Josiah seemed pretty content to be with me too.

"This is it," I said, indicating the two-story house that I'd called home my entire life. It was set well back from the road and looked as if it had been there for ages. Part of the east wall was almost completely covered by ivy.

My mom was in the kitchen as we entered and was more than a bit surprised to see Josiah. I don't think I'd ever brought anyone, other than Kelly, home with me in my entire life. Mom was very friendly, however, and offered Josiah some of her chocolate chip and walnut cookies for which she was famous. We both took some and headed for my room. Josiah was very polite to my mother and I could tell it impressed her.

"Have a seat," I said.

Josiah awkwardly sat on my bed and looked around my room. There were pictures of soccer players all over the walls.

"You like soccer?" asked Josiah.

"Uh, yeah. I don't play on a real team or anything, but I like it."

"I played soccer at one time, football too, but I haven't done that for a long time," said Josiah almost wistfully.

"I do a little track," I said. "I'm not much good at most things, but I'm pretty fast. I guess it's from running from the twins all the time."

"The twins?" asked Josiah.

"Yeah, those guys that you got off me. You're new, so you don't know yet, but they bully everyone they can. Some boys call them *the terrible twins.*"

"I can see why they would."

I looked at Josiah for a moment. I couldn't believe that he was in my house, sitting on my bed. I was happy. He was like a real friend.

"So what are your parents like?" I asked.

"They were very nice," said Josiah sadly. I caught onto the "were" very quickly.

"I'm sorry."

"It's okay. They died a long time ago. It's really pretty hard for me to even remember them most of the time, except sometimes, when I can see them in my mind just as they were." He smiled, but it was a very sad smile.

"So who do you live with?"

"I have…, well I guess you could call him a guardian. He's not related to me or anything, but he's like a parent."

"Cool, maybe I can meet him some time."

Josiah looked disturbed by the idea.

"I don't think that will be possible," he said. "He just doesn't like anyone around. Don't get me wrong, he's very nice, but we have an unspoken agreement that I don't bring anyone home with me."

"Oh, okay." I couldn't help but be just a bit hurt, although I probably should not have been.

I got up and stepped to my dresser to put away my wallet. I froze. I was looking into the mirror and I noticed something rather peculiar. I could see me. I could see the room. I could see the bed. I could *not* see Josiah.

I looked back over my shoulder and he was sitting on the bed where he had been all along. I looked back at the mirror. I could see the part of the bed he was sitting on. I could even see where it was pressed down from his butt being on it, but I couldn't see Josiah himself. I just stood there gawking for a moment.

Josiah got up quickly and moved to the chair at my desk. I stared at him for a moment. His eyes were a bit wide and he seemed uncomfortable. He was chewing on his fingernails.

"You know…I hate to cut things short, but I really need to be getting home," he said. "It was fun. Maybe we can do this again sometime."

In mere moments he was out of my room and out the front door. He seemed frightened. I watched out my window as he walked away. When he was out of sight, I stepped to my bed and sat exactly where

Josiah had sat. I turned to the mirror and saw my own eyes staring back at me. I just sat there in shock. What was going on?

CHAPTER 6

A Close Brush with Death

For the entire thirteen years of my life, the little community in which I lived had been the most boring in all the world. The front-page news often had something to do with livestock, or such exciting events as a water line being repaired or a garage being erected. I'd long thought that we could all use a bit of excitement. When it finally arrived, however, I was no longer so sure.

"Oh, that's dreadful," said Kelly to one of her friends as I entered school on Monday morning.

"What's dreadful?" I asked.

"This," she said, handing me the paper. I read it with astonished eyes.

LOCAL MAN KILLED BY WILD DOG

> *Twenty-three year old Nate Cartman was found dead early Sunday morning in the woods to the west of town. Bite marks on his face and neck were made by some kind of dog, or dogs. Authorities are warning residents to be on the lookout for any suspicious looking animals and are to report their presence immediately. It is believed that rabies is likely involved…*

"Oh, it's just horrible," said Kelly. "I heard my dad talking about it last night. His friend is with the police department you know. He said Nate's neck was ripped open. It must have been a horrible sight. I don't want to even think about it."

The gruesome killing was about all anyone could think or talk about. Even Josiah knew about it when I met him at lunch, and he seemed to speak with no one but me. Josiah was nearly always cool and dispassionate, but he seemed unusually upset by the killing and didn't want to discuss it.

Bry eyed Josiah coldly as he walked by and Josiah returned his stare. I felt oddly cold myself as they gazed at one another. It was clear they did not like each other at all. Bry was jealous of Josiah without a doubt and I supposed Josiah had picked up on his dislike of him, and started to dislike him in return. Josiah left lunch early and I was left to sit by myself. I wondered if the two of us were doing so well after all. We'd got on well on Friday evening, but Josiah seemed distant once again.

"It's not wise to hang out with him," said a voice behind me when I'd nearly finished my lunch. Even before I turned, I knew it was Bry, back again.

"What'd you mean?" I asked.

"I think you already know the answer. Haven't you noticed something very odd about Josiah, something unnatural?"

I stared at Bry blankly. There was a great deal that was odd about Josiah, but I didn't see what it had to do with anything.

The twins passed the table and looked at Bry and I. They acted strangely, almost fearful. It was not a look I was accustomed to seeing on their faces. It was quite out of place.

"They understand," said Bry, nodding toward the twins as they walked on. "You'll understand too, soon enough."

Bry left me rather confused. I was a bit taken back by his sudden interest in conversing with me, and even more taken back by his words. He didn't seem friendly, and yet it was as if he were sincerely trying to warn me about something. It was all very peculiar and strange.

❦   ❦   ❦

I caught up with Josiah just after school that very same day. It seemed the unpleasantness at lunch was forgotten. He was just as friendly as he had been on Friday. We got twisters again from Clark's, but this time we walked around town and the park while we ate them. Josiah seemed glad of my company, but there was a part of him that was still reserved. He was still a bit stiff around me. I guess that shouldn't have come as a surprise. After all, we hadn't known each other long and he was quite reclusive. It was a wonder he was talking to me at all. He sure didn't have anything to do with anyone else. He kept everyone at arm's length, except for me.

I almost felt that he could read my mind. No sooner had I thought about how he kept everyone at a distance than Josiah looked at me with sadness. I could feel him drawing back from me, although he said nothing. His eyes suddenly seemed empty and distant. I almost thought he was about to cry.

"I really should go home," he said.

I nodded, not trusting myself to speak for the moment. There was a knot in my throat and I was fighting to keep tears from welling up in my eyes. Josiah looked at me sadly, turned on his heel, and left me standing alone. A single tear ran down my cheek.

I sat down on a bench. The park suddenly seemed a lonely place. I could hear boys playing basketball in the distance and see little kids on the swings, but I might just as well have been on an island, hundreds of miles from the nearest living soul. My heart felt cold.

I gazed around at the flowers, the newly mown grass, and the trees, but their beauty was lost on me. It was as if I couldn't really see them. A lot of people seemed to go through their entire lives like that—looking at things, but not really *seeing* them. I had the rare gift of almost always being aware of all the little things that made life so enjoyable, but for the moment, it was gone. It left me feeling distant, even from myself. Trying to be Josiah's friend wasn't easy. After every forward step of progress, there was a step back. I sighed. Why couldn't things just work out like I wanted?

It wasn't time for work, but I headed for Mr. Diggory's place anyway. I loved visiting his home; it was an enchanting little world all onto itself, quite unlike any other. Basil was so kind that he made me feel happy and content, even when my spirits were low. I needed that just now. Basil was also the most interesting person ever; spending time with him was more entertaining that watching television or reading a good book.

I was at the far edge of town, near where Josiah lived, and cut through the woods on a whim. There wasn't a need to hurry and I thought being in the forest might improve my mood. I was wrong. I wasn't feeling very good as I walked among the trees. Just as in the park, I wasn't able to take pleasure in all the little things—like the birds and the tiny purple flowers. I was too troubled. Why did Josiah have to pull back from me just when we seemed to be getting close? He'd done it twice now. We got on well for a while, and then he just kind of closed up. What was so wrong with me that I couldn't make even one friend? I wasn't ready to give up on Josiah yet, but things were not looking so good. It was a bitter disappointment coming on the heels of my great hope. The contrast made it all the more unsettling.

I hated disappointment. Sometimes I felt like my life was filled with it. I had hoped that Josiah would be different from the others. None of the boys at school wanted to be my friend. I was small and not any good at sports. I wasn't "cool"—so they didn't want me around. Guys like Bry were the cool ones. They were at the top of the social ladder. I wasn't even on the ladder. Why did everything have to be a big popularity contest? I hated it. Sometimes, I felt like an outcast. Josiah had been a ray of hope, but even he didn't want to spend time with me.

The forest grew unusually quiet. I didn't notice it for a while because I was so lost in thought. The birds had even stopped singing. I suddenly grew fearful as if I could sense something that I could neither hear, nor see. I had the most overpowering feeling that I was not alone. I jerked my head one way, then another, but I could detect nothing. Some basic instinct warned me of danger, even if my customary senses couldn't perceive it. The hair on the back of my neck was standing on end. Someone was there, or something. I spun on my heel—and screamed. A great hairy shape was flying toward me. It was so close all I could see was a blur of fur. I didn't even have time to raise my arms to fend it off. It hit me in the chest and knocked me down before I could even get a good look at it.

I could hear jaws snapping and a horrible growl as I fought to fend off whatever it was with my arms. Its breath was putrid. In such close quarters all I could see was teeth and hair. I was panic-stricken. All I could think about was poor Nate Cartman and how I was about to end up just like him. I fought to keep the beast away from my throat, but I knew I was too weak to succeed. Whatever it was, it was powerful and strong, much too strong for me.

I was disorientated and terrified, screaming for help that could not come in time. It was a nightmare become real. I felt myself falling into blackness. I thought I saw a boy for a moment, Josiah, but it couldn't be for in his place the next moment was a great black wolf. Images faded in and out and I couldn't be sure what was real, and what was not. My thoughts slipped away. My last lucid thought was that if this was dying, then it wasn't so bad.

❦   ❦   ❦

I opened my eyes. The first thing I realized was that I was not dead. My heart still beat in my chest and my breath still passed through my nose and mouth. My hands reached for my neck and it was quite whole. Indeed, I didn't seem harmed at all. I wasn't sure how long I'd been unconscious, but it couldn't have been more than a few minutes because the sky was still light.

I was trembling with fear. I pulled myself up and looked about me. There was no sign of the wolf. The only evidence that I'd been attacked was the disturbed leaves on the forest floor. I was entirely befuddled and disorientated. I had no idea why the wolf hadn't finished me off. By all rights I should have been laying dead and mangled on the forest floor. Instead, it was as if nothing had happened at all. I knew full well that it wasn't some dream or fantasy. My hand found a small rip at the collar of my shirt. Here was evidence that the attacking beast was no product of my imagination. But why had it not killed me? I scurried for the edge of the woods in fear. I was unharmed, but I didn't want to stick around and give the beast a second chance. I made straight for Mr. Diggory's house. I knew that there I would be safe.

Basil gazed at me as I entered and I had little doubt he could sense my fearful, agitated state. He didn't press for information and I was relieved; for some reason I was not comfortable telling him what had just happened. Basil made me some orange spice tea and sat with me and had a cup himself.

"A good cup of tea can cure most any ailment of the body, mind, or heart," said Basil. The tea did help to calm my nerves, as did Basil's quiet presence.

Taylor and Devon sniffed at me curiously, and I wondered if they could not smell the wolf. I scratched them behind the ears and they growled contentedly. I began to feel more at ease as I sat in Basil's home. It wasn't long before I felt less shaky.

I pondered Basil as I sat across from him. He was forever cheerful and gave the impression of a kindly old man, but I suspected there was much more to him than was visible on the surface. I could sense a great strength within him and I had little doubt that he could face down nearly any danger. Just being near him made me feel safe.

I inhaled the spicy scent of my tea and gazed about me. Basil's house was so homey and comfortable that I felt like curling up and taking a good nap. It had an earthy feel to it; no doubt that atmosphere was created largely by the many herbs hanging from the ceiling and walls, as well as from the live plants that brought a bit of the outdoors indoors. It was a place where nothing seemed to ever change. I had the notion that if I went away a hundred years and came back, all would be as it was on the day I left. Just being there made me feel secure.

Basil set me to work replenishing his store of herbs from several packages that lie on the table. I refilled one glass jar after another as Basil busied himself with the pot on the stove. When my task was finished, Basil took me outside and we weeded the garden, while he taught me more about herb-lore. By the time we were done, I was feeling much better.

Later, as I was picking up fallen limbs from Basil's small yard, I thought once more about Josiah. My feelings for him were strong and growing stronger. Even being attacked by a wolf didn't force my thoughts away from him for long. I was drawn to him. Things weren't going so well between us, but I had no choice but to keep trying. Part of me wished that I didn't feel for him so strongly, but I couldn't help that. I just hoped that, somehow, things would work out.

🍁   🍁   🍁

I worked long into the night doing my homework, then undressed and crawled into bed. I was tired, but did not sleep soundly. I had nightmares of attacking wolves, whole packs of them lunging at my throat, trying to kill me. It all seemed so real, as dreams often do, that I was still frightened when I awakened the next morning.

It wasn't until I'd showered and wiped the steam from the bathroom mirror that I noticed the two bite marks on my neck. They were there, plain to see—two little marks about two or three inches apart. It was a wonder I hadn't noticed them before. I guess I was too shaken and terrified to take note of them after the struggle, and then my shirt had hidden them. They weren't very deep anyway. I guess I was lucky. That wolf could have ripped my throat out, just like it did to Nate. I'd gotten away with the tiniest of bites. Still, it was frightening, coming that close to what could have been my death. I still couldn't understand why it hadn't finished me, but maybe it had rabies like they said. Maybe it was so out of its mind that it attacked and retreated without reason.

    I paused, suddenly very afraid. If the wolf had rabies…The wound was not deep, but it had bitten me. What if I had rabies too? I didn't like that thought at all. I'd heard something about the treatment for rabies, something about 31 shots in the stomach, excruciatingly painful shots. I wondered if I should tell anyone I'd been bit. Then again, maybe that was not a wise idea. If I told my parents, they might make me get the shots whether or not, just to be safe. No, I'd wait and see. Surely I could tell if I was getting it. I frowned. I was more ill at ease than ever before. Why did I have so many problems? What had I done to deserve everything that was happening to me?

CHAPTER 7

❦

Warnings from All Sides

I sat with Josiah the next day at lunch, but he seemed distant. It was almost as if we were back where we'd started. He talked little, and volunteered nothing. He looked at me almost fearfully. Josiah had always acted a bit queer, but he was odder than ever. It seemed my entire world had become strange.

Why couldn't anything ever be easy? Why couldn't things just work out the way I wanted? Everything in life was so complicated. All I wanted was a friend, and maybe a boyfriend. Was that too much to ask? Josiah was obviously lonely. He needed a friend. So why couldn't he be *my* friend? Why couldn't he just jump at the opportunity and have fun with me? I knew wanting him to be my boyfriend was a bit much, but why couldn't he at least be my friend? What was so freaking hard about that?

🍁   🍁   🍁

The strangeness of my life only intensified. As I was putting away my books at the end of the day, I felt someone standing behind me. I thought perhaps it might be Josiah and grew hopeful. Perhaps he wanted to hang out and all would be as it had been. When I turned around, however, it was not Josiah. It was Bry.

"We need to talk," he said quite seriously. I was almost afraid I was in some kind of trouble. I was almost afraid he was going to drag me off the way the twins sometimes did and hurt me. He didn't seem in that sort of mood, however, he seemed edgy and almost afraid.

"What do we need to talk about?" I asked.

"That," he said, pointing to the collar of my shirt.

"Huh?"

"I saw the bite marks this morning, Graham, and you aren't the only one that has them."

I swallowed hard. I thought I'd kept them covered up better than that. I followed Bry as he led me out of the school. He took me out to the football field and we sat on the bleachers. The light wind whipped his hair around. Bry was so incredibly handsome that he made my heart race, even when I was fearful that he might do me harm.

Bry turned his head one way, then another, unnecessarily checking to made sure we were alone. The football field and bleachers were quite obviously deserted.

"How did you get that?" he asked.

"I was, uh, attacked by a wolf."

"Weird," said Bry "especially since the last wolves around here died out over a hundred and fifty years ago."

"I think maybe it's like a pet or something that got away from someone."

"Could be," said Bry, as he picked a blade of grass and twisted it with his fingers. "Or could be it's something else." He stared deeply into my eyes, holding my gaze with his.

"What'd you mean?"

Bry didn't answer. He was gazing intently over my shoulder. He stood. I turned. Although I had not seen him draw near, Josiah was standing there, almost as if he'd appeared from nowhere. There was a look of anger in his eyes as he looked at Bry that he could not quite disguise. I glanced over and noted that Bry returned his look with one much the same.

"Hey, Josiah, how are you?" I asked. Josiah had been out of sorts at lunch and I hoped he was better.

"I'm quite fine," he said with his British accent. His eyes did not leave those of Bry and they were icy.

"Come on," said Bry, pulling me away from the bleachers and toward the woods.

"Wait," said Josiah, grabbing my shoulder and stopping me. "I, uh, I've really got to talk to you."

"Right now?" I asked. "Can't this wait?"

"Push off!" said Bry in a none too friendly tone.

Josiah glared at him.

They stood there on the edge of fighting. I wasn't quite sure what was up. There was a tension in the air I could nearly feel. I wasn't quite sure what to do. I didn't want them to fight.

"Listen, why don't we all go get some ice cream or something?" I suggested. I knew it was kind of lame, but I had to do something. From the way they were looking at each other, Bry and Josiah weren't about to go eat together.

"I'm sorry about this," Josiah said to me. "But I really need to talk to you. I wouldn't ask if it wasn't so important."

"Do you mind?" I asked Bry. I was quite sure he did, but he gave me a friendly smile.

"Go ahead," said Bry. "Just make sure you stay where others can see you, in public. It's not a good idea to be alone. I'll catch up with you later. Be careful." He was still eyeing Josiah. I couldn't figure out why he was warning me not to go anywhere alone with Josiah, but it frightened me. Bry gave Josiah one last unpleasant look and walked away.

"Now what's so important?" I asked.

Josiah held up his finger, indicating I should wait a minute. He watched Bry departing. Only when he had disappeared from view did Josiah speak.

"I didn't want him to hear," he said.

Josiah was certainly paranoid. He'd waited far longer than was necessary to start talking. No one had hearing *that* good, did they?

"So talk," I said, more than a little impatient. I really liked Josiah, but he had been acting especially odd and moody. I was also shaken by Bry's warning, vague as it was.

"You shouldn't hang around Bry. He's not what you think."

"What do you mean?"

"I can't really explain it to you, but please, stay away from him."

"Josiah, I really like you. I'm hoping we can become good friends, but you don't even know Bry. I've never even seen you talk to him—not once. How could you possibly know anything about him? I think you'd better tell me the real reason you're trying to keep me away from him."

"I…I can't do that," said Josiah. "You just have to trust me."

I was not happy at all. Why was he so odd and suspicious? I was beginning to wonder if I'd made a wise chose in trying to befriend him. He acted like someone with something to hide and I was beginning to take Bry's warning more seriously.

"Listen, I'm not all that fond of Bry, but I don't see any reason to avoid him," I said. "I'm not going to ignore him because you've got some bad feeling about him or whatever it is. I appreciate your concern, but you are worrying for nothing. You can't even tell me why you think I should stay away from him, or you just won't. I need a very good and clear reason to do what you're asking. Are you going to give me one?"

"Graham, please. I can't. Just please stay away from him."

"No," I said. "I'm not going to do that."

"Graham, I know I have no right to ask, but please."

"Get off it, Josiah, and stop bothering me about it!" I was growing very cross and frightened, and was practically yelling. I could tell I hurt Josiah, but at the moment I didn't care.

"I'm going home," I said. "Thanks for ruining my evening. From now on keep your nose out of my business."

I turned on my heel and walked away fuming. A part of me wanted to cry. I felt like I'd just ruined things with Josiah. I wasn't even quite sure why I'd done it. I had overreacted. Then again, Josiah couldn't give me one good reason for staying away from Bry, and Bry was going out of his way to warn me about Josiah.

I needed to think and walk off some of the stress I was feeling, so I walked around town for a while. I always walked when something was bothering me, or when I just had something to think about. This was certainly one of those times.

I found myself walking out of town, but not toward home. Instead, my steps led me in the direction of the old amusement park. I pushed aside limbs and undergrowth as I drew ever nearer. The forest that surrounded the park was silent, except for the occasional call of a bird or some other sound of nature.

I misjudged and came out south of the park, on the disused road that led to its gates. The road was covered with tree limbs and fallen leaves that had never been cleared away. The towering roller coaster was in clear view now, as was another ride that had been hidden by the trees until I'd drawn close. Mere moments seemed to have passed when I was standing before the gates—locked tight with a massive chain. The sign above the entrance had come loose and one end was hanging down. It still read *Forest Grove Amusement Park*, just as it had when I visited it last—all those years ago.

The park felt forlorn and lonely. Through the locked gates I could see the ticket booths, once the gateway into a fantasy realm of joy, now forgotten and empty; their windows fogged and dusty. Just beyond them I could make out the skeet-ball building. I could remember being there with my parents. I wasn't old enough to be much good, but Dad helped me and we eventually won enough tickets for a small teddy bear. I still had it somewhere in my closet at home.

The gates were too tightly chained for me to squeeze through, so I followed the fence around the perimeter of *Forest Grove*. I turned the corner and headed north, gazing at the buildings that once housed the gift shop, a little museum, and the main dining area. I continued on, passing the spot where the spider ride once stood. That's what I called it; I couldn't remember what it was really named, but it was one of those rides that looked kinda like a big spider, or an octopus. I remembered how it looked harmless enough, but scared the crap outta me and just about made me hurl. I was only six or seven then, but still—it was scary. The ride was gone now; only the covered turnstile remained. That's one ride I didn't miss.

A little further on I could see the tracks of the little miniature railroad that traveled around the top of a hill at the far northern edge of the park. It was a tiny little train, kid-sized, that passed Mother Goose characters. I smiled to see that the characters were still there, standing frozen in time. The tracks were still there too, rusty and disused.

I turned to the west and passed the old picnic area. The long low pavilions still stood with dozens of picnic tables under them, but all was still. It gave me a lonely feeling inside to think of all the people that had been there enjoying themselves—eating, drinking, laughing. Now, they were all gone. I got the strangest feeling that I was alone in the world just then. It was as if everyone else had gone and I was the only person left on the entire planet. I yearned for someone to talk to. I thought about Josiah.

Before I reached the raft ride I found it, the opening in the fence. A small bit of the fence had been pried back from the pole and there was just enough room for a small person to squeeze through. I had no trouble at all.

I walked along the paved paths of the park, passing the old drink stand that sold souvenir cups, pretzels, and other treats. I could remember standing in line there for cotton candy. I liked the blue best—it was so much better than the pink.

I brushed last fall's leaves off a bench and sat down near the old drink stand, facing what was once an outdoor theatre where high school kids wore flashy costumes and sang pop tunes. The canvas roof was gone, the benches empty. The stage was covered in leaves and moss and the background fading, losing its glitter.

Down the hill and off to the left stood the Tilt-A-Whirl, rusting and disused. Beside it was the funnel cake stand and beyond them both was the great roller coaster, now silent. Perhaps it was because I'd been there when the park was filled with life and laughter, but it seemed such a lonely place. Maybe it was I who brought the loneliness with me. Josiah confounded me. One moment I thought of us as friends and the next I wasn't so sure I'd ever talk to him again. I'd dreamed so long of having another guy for a friend that I'd never thought there could be problems once I found one. I'd always imagined I'd make a friend and then we'd be like Tom Sawyer and Huck Finn. Real life wasn't like that, though. Josiah seemed in great need of a friend and yet he'd resisted me for so long. When at last he began to let me in, he quickly pulled away again, almost as if teasing me; holding out his friendship, then pulling it away again.

I wondered what was up with Josiah and Bry. Each warned me off the other. Bry's warnings made the most sense, but the very fact he bothered to care made the least sense. Bry hadn't so much as looked at me before Josiah came around. I had a sneaking suspicion his motive was envy of Josiah. Still, that didn't explain his warnings. Why should he care if I was friends with Josiah? Was my friendship such a prize? No one else wanted me, except Kelly. It wasn't like me hanging around with Josiah gave him some kind of advantage over Bry. The concern Bry expressed seemed genuine too. It was as if he was really worried about me. That in itself was confusing. Bry's motto had always seemed to be "If it's not happening to me, it doesn't matter." I sincerely doubted he'd turned over a new leaf, and yet, he seemed so sincere.

Josiah's warnings against Bry were so vague my instinct was to ignore them. If he was so earnest in his concern, why would he not explain himself? I felt as if he were attempting to create unreasoning fear within me to keep me away from Bry. But, why would he care if I hung around with Bry or not? It wasn't like Bry and I were buds. He'd merely talked to me now and then. It was almost as if Josiah was jealous of him, but if so, why didn't Josiah make more of an attempt to spend time with me? I couldn't figure any of it out. I definitely wasn't going to become a private detective when I grew up. I couldn't solve the simplest mystery.

I sighed. I closed my eyes and grinned. Despite it all, my heart felt full. I had this warm feeling inside when I thought about Josiah. He sure wasn't perfect, but I could feel myself falling for him. I just knew we could be the best of friends. I hoped for even more than that. I was treading through unfamiliar territory, but my feelings for Josiah were more than friendship. I couldn't help myself—I was falling in love.

What am I going to do with you, Graham Granger? I asked myself out loud. I was complicating my life with things I didn't understand and likely setting myself up for a fall. I knew in my heart the risk was worth it. I well remembered my life before Josiah; a life of loneliness and unfulfilled yearning. If we couldn't at least be friends, at worst I'd be back to my former life. That thought filled me with dread. Perhaps that was the real danger; exposing myself to something better, to a life of companionship that might not work out in the end. Having tasted that life, it would be that much harder if I had to go back to being alone. The potential reward was worth that risk. Even if the future didn't turn out like I wanted, I had the present. That's all life was really, a series of presents.

I hadn't left things very well with Josiah, but that could be mended. Perhaps I could even convince him to tell me why he so worried about me being around Bry. Who knew? No matter, I'd enjoy his friendship while I could.

I decided to save exploring the park further for another day. I didn't want to wander around that empty place alone. I wanted to be with others—with Josiah. I made my way back, through the opening in the fence, and back through the woods to town. It wasn't all that long before my feet had carried me to the town park once again.

I breathed in the fresh air. The park was a peaceful place with a beautiful lawn and a wonderful view of the little lake. It was a nice place to walk and think. Others were there, but they were doing their own thing and did not disturb me. I found their presence comforting. Unlike *Forest Grove* the town park was alive with activity.

I was so lost in my own thoughts that I was startled when someone reached out and grasped my arm. I'd nearly walked past without seeing him as he sat on a bench.

"Bry," I said, slightly surprised to see him.

"I've been looking for you. I was worried," he said.

"I'm sorry about Josiah. I don't know what his problem is."

"I do. So what did he say about me?" asked Bry.

"How do you know it was about you?"

"I could tell by the way he looked at me. Besides, I think I know what he's up to. I suppose he was trying to get you to stay away from me."

"Yeah, he was. He said you weren't what you seemed."

"What else did he say?"

"Nothing very specific, that's one reason I didn't listen to him. He seemed very determined that I avoid you. He seemed almost frightened for me."

"The dude does put up a good act. I'll give him that," said Bry. "I think he's the one you need to watch, however. I have some suspicions about Josiah. I think he's dangerous—very dangerous."

"What do you mean?" I asked.

Bry peered deeply into my eyes. "Haven't you noticed some peculiar things going on? And haven't you noticed some really odd things about Josiah? And I don't just mean the way he keeps to himself all the time either."

"Well, you'll think this is crazy, but there is something I noticed twice. No, it's too strange to tell you about. You'll just think I'm nuts or something."

"Try me."

"Well, we were in Clark's, and then I noticed it again at my house. He doesn't like mirrors. It's really weird and I'm sure there's an explanation, but I couldn't see Josiah in the mirror. I could see where he was sitting on my bed in my room, but I couldn't see *him*."

I felt like a real whacko telling Bry that. I just knew he'd think I was loony. He wasn't the least bit fazed, however.

"This is bad," said Bry, standing and nervously pacing back and forth. "I've had my suspicions, but this confirms it. Shit. I didn't know if I should even talk to you about Josiah, but now I'm glad we're talking. This is *very* bad."

"What do you mean?"

"Well, something weird is going on. No one is talking about it, but I've noticed. You aren't the only one with bite marks on your neck."

"I know. I saw the twins." I swallowed hard. What Bry was saying would have sounded crazy, if I hadn't been bitten too. "I don't see what this has to do with Josiah, however. A wolf bit me."

"That wasn't just a wolf and I don't think you got that bite when you think you did," said Bry. He looked at me fearfully, but I had the feeling he was afraid for me. "You'd better sit down."

We sat side by side on the bench. I peered at him curiously, intently aware of my own heart beating in my chest.

"What I'm going to tell you is going to sound really crazy, but listen to me okay? Even if you think I'm a complete lunatic, just humor me for a couple of minutes."

"All right," I said.

"If a wolf bit you, it wouldn't leave a mark like that," said Bry. "There would be a lot of marks from all those teeth. There is only one thing that leaves bite marks like that." He stopped, as if afraid to say more.

"What? What leaves bit marks like that?"

"A vampire," said Bry in a hoarse whisper.

I nearly laughed, but Bry was deadly serious.

"Before you call me crazy, think about it," he said. "Do you even remember the wolf biting you? Did you feel it? You know it would have hurt like hell."

"Uh, no. I don't remember," I said. Bry's words were making sense, and frightening me.

"Do you really think you could be bitten and not even know it, unless whatever bit you had a way to keep you from knowing? Josiah doesn't have a reflection in mirrors. Have you ever in your entire life heard of anyone, or anything, that doesn't have a reflection in a mirror? The only thing that doesn't have a reflection is a vampire. Vampires can transform themselves into wolves. I think he transformed from a wolf into a vampire, then bit you."

Bry was right about the lack of a reflection in the mirror, and about how I should have felt it when I got bit, but most of what he was saying was crazy. There were no vampires. He might as well have been talking about witches and wizards. Vampires just weren't real.

"Josiah goes out in the sunlight. Vampires can't do that," I pointed out. Bry wanted me to humor him, so I would, but he'd have to explain a few things.

"Movie vampires can't do that," said Bry. "Real vampires can. They can't look directly into the sun and bright sunlight hurts their eyes, but they can stay in sunlight for limited periods of time. It hurts them, but it doesn't destroy them, not unless they are in direct sunlight for quite a long time. If you don't believe me, ask Josiah to go to the beach with you and see what happens."

"And just how do you know these things about vampires?" I asked. I figured this question would get him. Monsters were kind of a hobby of mine and I'd read up on vampires, but I'd never heard some of the stuff he was telling me.

"Because my father is an expert on the occult. He's a university professor and has studied cases of real vampirism. I don't blame you for not believing me, but it's real. There is a lot of stuff that is real that you probably wouldn't believe."

That was true enough. In social studies, Mr. Preble had told us how everyone thought Marco Polo was making things up when he told them he had seen rock that burns. It sounded crazy to everyone, but he was talking about coal. I wasn't convinced, but I was open-minded.

"At least consider what I've told you," said Bry. "I'm worried about you. I know you probably don't believe me, but I'm certain now that Josiah is what I suspected. That's why he doesn't want you near me. Somehow he knows that I know about him. Keep your distance from him, Graham. Even if you don't believe me, stay away from him, for your own safety."

"Why do you suddenly care what happens to me? You sure didn't before."

"Listen, I know I can be a jerk. I'm know I'm kind of conceited and maybe don't pay much attention to a lot of people, but it doesn't mean I don't care. I don't want to see anyone get hurt, and you're…Well, I'm just afraid you'd be easy for him to hurt."

"Because I'm small?"

"Yes. Don't get mad. I'm not putting you down, but you are an easy target. I'm afraid he'll do something bad to you, Graham. He told you I'm not what I seem. It is *he* who isn't what he appears to be. If he bites you once more you'll become like him. Or he may decide to kill you. I don't want to see either of those things happen to you. Please, please stay away from him."

I was hurt by his comments about me being small, although I knew he didn't mean those words to hurt me. I didn't know what to say, or even to think. It was all so crazy and weird, but Bry was so sincere.

"Why don't I walk you home?" he said.

"No, it's all right. I'll be okay."

"Think about what I've said, and be careful."

I said goodbye and walked toward home. Bry didn't have to worry about me thinking about what he'd said. It was all I could think about.

I think I would have dismissed the whole idea of Josiah being a vampire if it hadn't been for a feeling I had deep down. Even before Bry had mentioned it, I'd been thinking it in the back of my head. It wasn't a thought I seriously entertained because it was so ludicrous, but why didn't he cast a reflection in the mirror? The more I thought about it, the more it didn't make sense that I couldn't remember when I'd been bit. Even though it wasn't a big bite, it should have hurt a lot.

I stopped dead in my tracks as a thought came to mind. The eyes—the eyes of the wolf—the eyes of Josiah; they were the same. They had the same shining blue eyes, an odd beautiful blue that I'd not seen before. The coincidences were beginning to pile up until they were no long coincidences. Too many pieces of the puzzle were beginning to fit. The impossible had become the possible.

CHAPTER 8

The Vampire at Griswold Jr./Sr. High

On Monday, I sat once more with Josiah at lunch, but I wasn't as talkative as I usually was. I couldn't get all that Bry had told me out of my mind. I just stared for a moment when Josiah looked up at me. His eyes locked on mine. They were the eyes of the wolf.

Josiah was very pale. He obviously didn't spend much time in the sun. Everything that Bry had said was making sense, as crazy as it all sounded.

"Hey, you want to go to the beach this weekend?" I asked. "We can swim and lay out in the sun and stuff." I watched carefully for his reaction. The question did make him seem very uncomfortable.

"Um, I can't really. I'll be busy, I think."

Maybe he really was busy, or maybe he turned me down because he couldn't go out in to the sun. I thought of something else.

"Hey, you've got to try this garlic toast. It's really, really good," I said, holding it out to him. Luckily we had spaghetti and garlic toast that day. I'd heard that vampires were repelled by garlic. Josiah did shrink away from it.

"No thanks," he said. "I never cared for it."

"Awww, come on, just one taste, for me," I said, looking at him with puppy dog eyes as I pushed it nearer to him. He leaned back to avoid it.

"No!" he said, angrily. "I told you I don't like it."

I backed off. The results weren't conclusive, but I was really starting to believe what Bry had told me. I was prepared for yet one more test, but I hesitated to do it. I was afraid.

Basil had told me that lemony smelling herb, lemon balm, was used to ward off vampires. I'd never once come across lemon balm in vampire lore. It was mentioned in many herb books, but that was it. Not one single book I could find on vampires made any mention of it at all. I was beginning to think that Basil was just foolin' me, but I found something in his own library that told me otherwise. The day after Bry had so earnestly warned me about Josiah, I browsed through Basil's books and found one called *Herbs For Combatting Dark Forces*. It stated quite clearly that contact with lemon balm caused vampires intense physical pain, as if it burned them. It also made them very ill and weak. It had the same effects as garlic, but was much, *much* stronger. I had found no mention of it anywhere else in vampire lore, but *Herbs For Combatting Dark Forces* was a *real* book, not one based on film versions of creatures of the night.

I had some lemon balm in my pocket. I'd brought it to test Josiah. I secretively slipped some into my hand and crushed it between my fingers. I reached out and took Josiah's hand as it sat on the table, putting the lemon balm directly on his skin. There was no need to wait for his reaction. It was immediate and violent. Josiah screamed and jerked his hand away so forcefully that he knocked his tray to the floor. He vaulted right up out of his seat. His face was contorted by pain as he looked at me with anger in his eyes. He was deathly pale, as if he were violently ill. I caught a quick glimpse of his hand. There were blistering welts where the lemon balm had touched him. If I had any doubts that Josiah was a vampire, or that lemon balm was a potent weapon against the creatures of the night, they were erased.

Josiah looked almost as if he were about to attack me, but was in too much pain to do so. I'd never seen such an intense look of pain on anyone's face before. Tears even streamed down his cheeks. He leaned toward me, but I got up quickly. I was afraid he was going to come after me right there in front of everyone. I pulled the rest of the lemon balm out of my pocket and held it where he could see, warding him off. He came no closer. I picked up my tray and left. Everyone in the cafeteria was gawking at us. I'd created quite a scene.

The rest of the day seemed unreal. Vampires were fictional. They were only found in books and movies. I was faced with something that could not be, and yet it was real. Basil knew everything there was to know about herbs and he'd said that lemon balm warded off vampires. That book I'd read said the same. Josiah had reacted violently when I touched him with some. His reaction had been immediate too. I'd barely touched him when he screamed. Skin didn't blister like that either, not without being burned. I considered that maybe he was just terribly allergic to lemon balm, but even if he was, his skin would not have blistered like that instantly, and it certainly wouldn't have caused him such intense pain. I was pretty allergic to poison ivy and got little blister-like places on my skin from it, but it took a day or so to do that, and it was never as bad as what I'd seen on Josiah's hand.

It was all adding up. What Bry had told me was just plain crazy, except for one thing—it was true. My mind wanted to reject it, but there was no denying reality.

❧   ❧   ❧

As I was pulling books out of my locker just after school, I stiffened. I felt someone looking at me. I turned to see Josiah nearly on top of me. I slammed my locker shut and backed away.

"Stay away from me!"

"Graham, I just want to talk to you." He kept edging closer. My heart was beating wildly. I kept backing away. I wasn't going to let him touch me. I wasn't going to let him get a hold of me. I'd seen how strong he was—unnaturally strong. It was further proof of what he was, as if I needed any.

"Stay back!" I said. "I've still got it!" I reached into my pocket and pulled out the wilted plant. There were others still in the hallway, but I was afraid he'd attack me anyway. I knew what he was and, more importantly, he knew that I knew. I was in mortal danger.

"You don't understand," he said.

"I understand plenty. Now get away from me!"

I turned and ran. Josiah did not follow me. I was shaken, and afraid. I kept running. I felt like my life had become a nightmare. The boy I'd hoped would be my friend had turned out to be a monster. It really was like one of those dreams where someone turns into someone else and everything is crazy, but it all makes sense in the dream. I wondered if maybe I wasn't in a dream. Everything that had happened had a dream-like quality to it. Maybe I'd wake up soon and laugh at the crazy shit I'd been dreaming. Somehow I knew that I wasn't dreaming, however. I could always tell. It didn't matter how real my dreams seemed, some little part of me always knew I was dreaming. There was no little part of me telling me I was in a dream now. What I was experiencing was reality.

I kept right on running until I reached my oak tree in the forest. I sat at the foot of it and cried. I was frightened and felt very alone and miserable. I was terrified that Josiah was going to get me, but that wasn't the worst of my pain. My dreams of having him for a friend, and possibly a boyfriend, were destroyed. My heart ached. The one time I had the courage to reach out to someone, it ended in disaster. I'd gone looking for a friend and I'd found a monster. Somehow, having someone I cared about turn out to be something so horrible made it all the worse. How could I have been so wrong about Josiah? How could my own heart have lied to me?

I was startled by a noise overhead, but it was just Angelica landing on a limb. I wiped the tears from my eyes.

"You scared me," I told her. She looked back at me blinking. I felt a little better with her there. It was as if she were my protector.

I knew it wasn't wise to stay were I was for long. Josiah might come after me, even though it was still afternoon. I didn't feel safe outside anymore. I knew for sure that I wouldn't be going outside after dark. When night fell, Josiah would no doubt be after me, either as himself or the wolf. I wasn't sure which I feared most.

I got up and walked toward Basil's house. Angelica took off from her perch and followed me. She'd never done that before. She didn't leave me until I was walking up the old, familiar lane.

Basil greeted me with his usual smile, and a steaming cup of strawberry tea. Taylor and Devon jumped on me and covered my face with kisses. I felt safe for the first time that day. For some reason I felt that Basil could protect me from even vampires. That thought made me remember how he'd mentioned them casually, and about the books in his library. Basil was probably the one person that might be able to tell me something useful.

"What do you know about vampires?" I asked him.

Basil looked at me over his cup and raised an eyebrow. He gave me a curious look.

"Why do you ask?"

"I was just wondering, if someone wanted to protect himself against one, how would he do it?"

I thought about first asking him if they were real, but I had the feeling he wouldn't tell me if he knew. Instead I tried for something practical.

"Well, it's been said that garlic repels them quite successfully," said Basil. "And my herb books says lemon balm is very effective against them." He looked at me as if he knew I'd read that for myself, although I didn't know how he could know that.

"Then there is holy water of course and a few other less effective means."

"Okay," I said. "I was just wondering. I'm kind of curious about all that."

I had the feeling that Basil didn't believe me, but he accepted my explanation.

"Would you mind if I took some of that lemon balm home? Just to have it."

"Not at all my boy. It grows much faster than I can use it. In fact, let me make you some lemon balm tea right now. I think you'll like it and if vampires attack, you'll leave a bad taste in their mouth," he smiled and chuckled softly, but I almost felt as if he were protecting me in a way.

In a few minutes time I was sipping lemon balm tea. It tasted kind of lemony like I expected. The taste made me think of gardens and summer. I drank it down. It was good and it probably really would help protect me. I needed all the protection I could get.

Basil put me to work refilling jars of herbs from some of the dried bunches that hung around the kitchen. I had to strip the leaves from the stems, then crush them and stuff them in the jars. Basil helped me identify the herbs that stumped me. I could identify some of them from their scent, but that was about the only way I could tell which herb was which. I couldn't do it from just looking at them. Most herbs looked pretty much the same when they were all dried up. It was a rather pleasant late afternoon, much better than my uncomfortable and frightening day.

Before I left I gathered a fair sized bunch of lemon balm and took it home with me. The first thing I did when I got to my room is divide it into smaller bunches. I hung one by each window and one by the door. I also put a little bunch on each corner of the bed and made a little bag of it that I hung around my neck. I closed the blinds tight. The last thing I wanted to see in the night were eyes peering at me.

I busied myself with homework; the sound of the pen scratching away on the paper was comforting and familiar. I even worked well ahead in my studies. I'd do anything to keep my mind off my topsy-turvy world. I yearned to seek escape with sleep, but I feared I'd never get the chance to wake up again. I was afraid that Josiah would come for me in the night. I knew what he was and that put me in great danger. I knew he couldn't let me live with that knowledge. Sooner or later, he was bound to get me, unless I found a way to get him first. I wished that I'd asked Basil about ways to kill vampires. Maybe Bry would know. I wondered if a stake through the heart is what it would take, like in the movies, or if it was something totally different. I was hoping it was different. I really didn't think I could drive a stake through anyone's heart. I wasn't about to try it without finding out for sure. So much of vampire lore was just made up and I was dealing with the real thing!

I grew very sleepy and my eyes began to hurt, but still I resisted sleep. Even if Josiah didn't come for me, I feared that I'd have horrible nightmares. Dreams like that could be almost as bad as reality. I'd had some really nasty ones in the past, dreams so bad I woke up shaking.

I fell asleep at my desk. I awoke there sometime late in the night and hobbled to my bed without completely waking up. I went back to sleep thinking how much more warm and comfortable my bed was than the desk. Luckily, no vampire came for me while I was unconscious and no bad dreams troubled my sleep.

CHAPTER 9

※

Desperate Measures

I got dressed and had buttered toast with strawberry jam for breakfast on Saturday morning. I watched a little television to kill some time, then I headed for Basil's about 11. I had some yard work to do there and some errands to run. Basil greeted me with a smile as always, and his two little dogs pawed me and licked at my face. Basil poured us both cups of steaming blueberry tea and we talked a little before I started work.

As we sat there over our cups of tea, Basil looked at me oddly for a few moments, giving me the kind of look I'd expect if I had my shirt on backwards or something. He didn't say anything, however, and the look was gone as quickly as it had come. I didn't think any more of it. I sat and sipped my tea. It was good tea. I'd never had blueberry before.

A few minutes later I was out mowing the lawn. It was sunny and hot. Within just a few minutes, my shirt was getting wet with sweat and sticking to my skin. I pulled it off and hung it on the porch railing. It felt good to have the sun beating down upon my shoulders. It made me feel safer too. I didn't think Josiah could get me when it was so very bright out.

The sun seemed especially bright and hurt my eyes. I wished that I had brought my sunglasses, but I was more than willing to do a little squinting if I could be safe from vampires.

I actually enjoyed mowing the lawn. I never cared that much for it at home, but it was different at Basil's somehow. Everything was different here. It was almost as if I was in another world when I was at Basil's home. Instead of thinking of it as a job, I just enjoyed the sun on my back and the scent of newly mown grass. If I tried hard enough, I could enjoy just about anything. It didn't take too much effort to enjoy mowing. It was such a pretty day that my spirits were lifted. I was done soon enough in any case. I put the mower away, slipped my shirt back on, and headed back inside.

The coolness of the house was refreshing. I was almost chilly in my damp shirt. Basil asked me to do a little dusting, as it was one of his least favorite things to do. Once I started, I could tell dusting was something he didn't do often. There was a thick layer of dust on just about everything.

Taylor and Devon kept jumping for the dust rag; they were crazy over it and the delighted expressions on their faces made me giggle. Their tails wagged furiously, their eyes sparkled, and they panted as if they'd been running. Dusting could have been a dull task, but not with those little dogs around. Taylor made a spectacular jump and got a hold of the rag; forcing me to wrestle him for it. Devon jumped in and latched onto it too. I thought they were going to take it away from me. Basil laughed when he saw us and rescued me by bring the boys some doggy biscuits. They left me in peace while they chewed on them.

I spent a lot of time dusting the bookshelves. It was the first time I'd had a chance to get a good, close look at Mr. Diggory's books. There were lots of shelves all loaded down with ancient tomes. Some of them looked extremely old, like they'd fall apart if I just looked at them. I gingerly dusted around those.

I read some of the titles on the spines and found that most of the books were very odd indeed. There were a great many on herbs, which didn't surprise me in the least, but there were others that I didn't expect to find there, or anywhere else for that matter. As I dusted I read the titles. There was *Cromwell's Magic Potions and Amulets, 1,001 Best Known Antidotes, The Big Book of Curses and Counter-Curses, Advanced Transmutation, Great Wizards of the 19th-20th Centuries, Self Defense Against Vampires & Ghouls, Hertwig's Book of Simple (But Useful) Spells*, and lots more that were even more odd. There were even books in languages that I couldn't make out, written with characters I'd never seen. Every single book was either about herbs or something to do with magic or vampires. It was the most fascinating library I'd ever seen in my life.

I had the strongest urge to try and slip out with *Hertwig's Book of Simple (But Useful) Spells* and see just what it was all about, but I couldn't be dishonest with Basil like that. I'd have brought it back, of course, but it wasn't right to just take it. I thought that maybe I could ask if I could borrow it sometime. I decided to wait on that a bit.

What interested me most were all the books on vampires. I'd never seen so many before and I wondered if there was something within their pages that might be of help to me. Knowing more about what I was facing might even save my life.

Time flew by and soon I was done. I was kind of sorry. I was always reluctant to depart from Basil's house.

"Um, Mr. Diggory?"

"Basil," he said kindly.

"Yes, Basil…Could I borrow some of your books sometime, or look at them here or something?"

"Certainly, you can do either, Graham. Just be very careful. Some of them are quite old, fragile, and irreplaceable."

"Thank you," I said. I went over and picked out a couple books on vampires that I thought would be useful.

"Oh, before you go, I need to pay you."

"I almost forgot I get paid," I laughed.

"Well, I'm glad you enjoy your work. You should always do what you enjoy. You're quite valuable to me, however, and you definitely deserve to be paid well."

I walked away with a pocket bulging with cash. I had the most wonderful job in the entire world! I was paid quite a lot and even dusting could be exciting at the Diggory house. I'd never been to such an intriguing place before.

※　　　　※　　　　※

I didn't sit with Josiah at lunch the next day. I wasn't about to go anywhere near him. I saw him sitting all my himself in his usual place. I felt sorry for him for a moment, but then I remembered what he was, and what he'd done. I wondered how many of us he'd fed on. I wondered how many of my classmates had bite marks on their necks like mine that they couldn't remember getting. I also remembered Nate. Looking at Josiah, I just couldn't believe he'd killed him. There was little doubt about it, however. Josiah must have killed him as a wolf, just as he tried to kill me not so long ago. Josiah appeared to be just a fifteen-year-old boy, but he was much more than that.

How can I stop him? And can I stop him before he strikes again? I thought to myself. I'd starting reading through the books I'd borrowed from Basil, but so far I hadn't run across anything useful.

I asked Bry to meet me in the park right after work. I was usually finished at Basil's by six-thirty so I knew we'd have plenty of time to talk before dark. I wanted to make sure I was home by the time the sun went down. Josiah could go about in the daylight hours, but I figured he was less likely to attack in the daylight, especially when others were around. That's why I wanted to meet Bry in the park. There were always plenty of people there. At the very least there would be fifteen or twenty boys playing basketball on the courts. There was safety in numbers.

Bry was there waiting on me when I arrived. I had more errands to run for Basil than normal, so I was running just a little late. The sun was already beginning to sink in the sky, so I didn't waste any time and dove right in.

"You were right," I said. "About Josiah. I tested him. I touched him with some of this." I took some withered lemon balm out of my pocket and held it out to Bry.

"Lemon balm," he said.

"Yes. He screamed when I touched him with it and his hand looked all red and blistered. I had my doubts before, but not now. He's a vampire, all right."

Bry was gazing at me curiously, with a bemused, somewhat surprised look that I couldn't quite place.

"How did you find out about lemon balm?" he asked. "Almost no one knows about its protective properties against vampires."

"This cool guy I work for, Mr. Diggory, mentioned it, then I found it listed in one of his books. I'd never heard of it before and thought he might have been kidding, but I was curious, so I looked it up."

A wave of anger and fear darkened Bry's handsome face, but only for a fleeting moment. His expression relaxed and left me wondering if I'd imagined what I'd read in his features mere moments before.

"Well, I'm glad you know now. I'm glad you believe me. I was worried about you—really worried. One more bite and you'd be his, you'd become one of them."

"I'm really scared, Bry. He knows that I know what he is. I know he'll come for me. He has to, before I expose him."

"Exposing him might not be so easy. Who is going to believe you when you tell them he's a vampire? You know they'll just laugh."

"I've thought of that, but I can't just do nothing! Who knows how many people he's attacked? He could be making more vampires every night! This whole town could be crawling with them already. Hell, you could even be one by now. I don't know who to trust."

"You really think I'd be warning you against him if he'd already made me into a vampire? More likely, I'd be after you too. Besides, I'm not one, see." Bry pulled off his shirt and showed me his neck from every angle.

I was momentarily distracted. I'd spent a lot of time imaging what Bry looked like without a shirt and at last, I could see for myself. He was smooth and muscular. Just looking at his chest and the tight rows of abdominal muscle made me breathe harder. I totally forgot what we were talking about for a few moments. Bry was gorgeous.

It wasn't until he slipped his shirt back on that I came to myself. There wasn't a bite mark to be seen on his neck. Bry hadn't been bit. He wasn't one of them. Too bad I couldn't get a look at everyone's neck.

"So what are you doing to protect yourself?" asked Bry.

"I'm wearing this," I said, indicating the little bag of lemon balm that I'd attached to the gold chain around my neck. "I also have some on each window and the door to my room, as well as on each corner of my bed."

"Well, you should be safe at home at least," said Bry. "And that lemon balm hanging around your neck should keep him from attacking you. Unless he's a powerful enough vampire to endure the lemon balm long enough to rip your chain away."

"He could do that?" I said. I hadn't thought of that before. "Do you think he's powerful enough to do it?"

"I don't know. From what my father told me, it would take a very, *very* powerful vampire to be able to do it. It'd only take a second, but most couldn't manage it. Most couldn't bear to get nearly that close. You could more easily pick up a piece of white hot metal than a vampire could touch that."

"At lunch, it didn't seem to bother him until I got it really close. He didn't scream until I touched him with it."

"Yeah, that's right. I've been asking Dad some questions, and doing a little reading on my own since I learned Josiah's secret. You'd have to get within a foot for it to work on him. Of course, he has to get closer than that to bite, so it's very effective. Very few vampires would attack you while you're wearing that around your neck. It will protect you from any he's created recently for sure."

"Hey, I've got this on my chain, so why don't you take what I've got in my pocket?" I held the lemon balm toward him.

"No! You are the one he'll be after. You may need that. I couldn't live with myself if he got you because you'd given me the very thing that could have saved you. I won't allow it."

"But I'm worried about you. There is nothing to stop him from attacking you. You've been so kind to me. I don't want anything to happen to you either."

"Don't worry about me, Graham. I'm protected. See this ring I'm wearing." He showed me a gold ring with a dragon on it. "This ring is very, very old. It belonged to a slayer, to someone who spent his life destroying vampires. It has a spell on it. It will protect me even better than that herb will protect you."

"A spell? You expect me to believe that there is a magic spell that will protect you? This is reality Bry, we're not playing Dungeons and Dragons."

"You've already seen it work," he said, eyeing me. A slight grin curled up the edges of his mouth. "You've seen how Josiah looks at me—that look of hatred. He knows what I'm wearing. He knows what it is. And he knows he can't touch me." Bry seemed very superior as he spoke, as if he were invulnerable or something.

"Where'd you get it?"

"My Dad gave it to me. I can understand you not believing it's real. I thought dad just made up all that about it being magic, but then…I met Josiah and I *knew*."

I found it very hard to believe in Bry's magic ring, but what he said did ring true.

"So don't worry about me. No vampire will be putting the bite on me, I assure you. Not all of us are defenseless against them."

Bry suddenly looked more serious than ever before.

"Don't be frightened for me, Graham, and don't think you are in this alone. I'll help you. I've been thinking about it and there is something we can do to stop Josiah." Bry paused as if he was almost afraid to go on. "It won't be pleasant or pretty, but he has to be stopped. I'm willing to go it alone if I must, but I'd have a much better chance of succeeding if you helped."

I looked into his eyes. I know my own showed fear. My chest suddenly felt tight. I had a feeling I knew what Bry was going to say. I wasn't wrong.

"There's only one way to stop him. We have to kill him."

"Murder?" I asked. Bry had just told me what I feared he would. I didn't even want to hear it.

"He is not what he seems," said Bry. "Josiah is not a fifteen year old boy. He was once, but he ceased to be that long ago. He is a creature—a monster that feeds on the blood of others. He turns them into what he is, or kills them. He killed Nate and you can bet your life there will be more deaths. I'm sure Josiah has killed before. If he's been a vampire for long, he's killed dozens at least, maybe hundreds. He has no choice. By killing him, we'll save everyone he would have killed. One evil life to save many good lives. We'll be doing Josiah a favor, too, Graham. Do you really think he wants to live the life he's living? He's in pain, Graham. He experiences the torment of being a creature that must maim and murder to survive. He's trapped and only someone like you or I can free him.

"I know it won't be easy, but it has to be done, and there's no one else to do it. It's up to us. I'll understand if you just can't, but I need you, Graham. We all need you."

I just sat there in silence. I couldn't believe what Bry was telling me, or that I was listening and seriously considering it. It all seemed so unreal, so impossible, but I had the bite marks on my neck to remind me that this was no fantasy. I'd once befriended Josiah. I'd once hoped we could be friends forever, and much more than friends. Now I had no choice but to kill him. My heart ached.

"So...um...I'm not saying I'm in on this, but if we...you know...kill him, do we, like, drive a stake through his heart or what?"

"You've been watching a few too many vampire films," said Bry, almost laughing. "That stake through the heart bit doesn't work. You try that on Josiah and all you'll get is a very pissed off vampire. He's not really alive, not like us. To kill him, we have to cut off his head and burn it until there's nothing left but ashes, then we must take those ashes and spread them over holy ground, so that he has no chance of coming back."

"Cut off his head!" I squeaked, much too loudly. I lowered my voice conspiratorially, "You can't be serious!"

"I wish I wasn't. Believe me, Graham, I wish there was a simpler and less messy way, but we're dealing with reality here, not some Anne Rice novel."

"Are you sure? I mean, I've always heard..."

"Let me repeat myself," said Bry. "This is reality, not fantasy. Most of what you've heard about vampires is just made up nonsense. According to some legends, vampires can go days without feeding and the longer they go without blood, the more pale and "corpse like" they look. According to other myths, vampires can't tolerate typical food of any kind. You've seen Josiah eat normal food, so you know it's not true. Reality, Graham. R-E-A-L-I-T-Y, not fantasy. Got it?"

I nodded.

Bry looked around at the deepening shadows. "You'd better go home," he said. "Vampires are much more powerful in the dark. It isn't safe for you to be out, not even with me to help protect you."

"All right," I said rising. "You'd better get home too, just in case."

"I will, now get out of here." He smiled as we parted. I did too. It felt good to have an ally, someone to watch my back. Never in a million years would I have guessed it would be Bry Hartnett, the school hunk, Mr. Popularity himself. I never even dreamed he'd look at me, let alone look out for me as he was doing. Life was weird.

I scurried home in the growing darkness, fearful of every noise. Things had certainly worked out differently than I'd planned, or hoped. This wasn't at all what I had imagined when I'd starting getting close to Josiah. I'd had such hopes for his friendship, and now this. I couldn't shake the feeling that I was trapped in some screwed up dream, but there was no doubt that what I was experiencing was real. Dreams covered moments in time, not continuous weeks. It was too bad I wasn't just dreaming. Nothing would have made me happier than to wake up and have things go back to normal. There were far worse things than being lonely.

CHAPTER 10

Into the Vampire's Lair

I gave Josiah the cold shoulder at school and completely avoided him. Whenever he passed near me in the halls I felt as if a chill were running up my spine. I couldn't believe such a monster was walking the halls of my school undetected by nearly everyone. Josiah Huntington wasn't going to get within ten feet of me if I could help it, not until it was time for Bry and I to do what we had to do.

I still wasn't sure if I was going to help Bry. I knew that I should, but the thought of killing someone...I didn't like hurting anyone, or anything. Josiah was a monster, but still...I knew he had to be stopped, but I wasn't at all comfortable with the idea of killing him. It was either that, or allow him to continue to kill, so there really wasn't any choice. Even so, I kept thinking about it. I couldn't believe I was involved in such a thing. I wished that I was far, far away.

If having to kill him wasn't bad enough, the way we had to do it was disgusting. In movies, ramming a stake into a vampire's heart was a messy business, but actually cutting off his head...I gagged just thinking about it. I didn't see how I could possibly do something like that!

I was afraid for Kelly. Like many of the girls, she had a crush on Josiah. She was taken in by his good looks and "sexy voice" as she called it. She didn't know that his voice was a siren call for destruction. I needed to warn Kelly, but I couldn't tell her the truth without her thinking I was a lunatic. No, that'd be no good and she'd just ignore me. Instead of the truth, I lied. I told her that Josiah had turned nasty on me, that he'd harassed and threatened me. I did such a good job of lying that I think I weakened her crush on him. I hated lying, especially to someone who trusted me so much, but I had to protect her. It was for her own good.

When my path crossed that of Josiah, sadness clutched at my heart. The friendship I'd wanted with him was impossible. I thought of what might've been if he was just a normal guy. It was a terrible thing that he had to be destroyed. He certainly didn't appear to be a murdering monster; he seemed just a boy. That's what made him so very dangerous. He was cloaked in secrecy and none would ever guess what a fiend he truly was until it was too late. I knew I had to push aside the feelings I'd had for him and remember what he truly was. He was no boy. He was a killer, and worse than a killer.

It became easier to remember the dark side of Josiah at night. I lay in my bed nervous and often shaking with fear. Sometimes I woke up soaked with sweat. I had unpleasant dreams and nightly heard something at my window. I'm not sure if it was a dream, or real, but I could see the shadow of someone there and I knew that only the protective herb stood between me and a horrible fate. I shivered in my covers and prayed that the vampire would not be able to get into my room.

*   *   *

My fingers felt clumsy as I worked the combination to my locker. I messed it up three times before I got it open. I was too busy keeping an eye out for Josiah to pay attention to what I was doing. My hands even trembled slightly and I had this queasy feeling in the pit of my stomach. I didn't feel safe anywhere. Suddenly, everything in my life was frightening—even the mostly deserted hallway seemed sinister—it was a possible location for an attack. I opened my locker and a sheet of paper floated to the floor. I picked it up and read the small, tightly written note:

Graham,

Meet me in the graveyard at 5 p.m.

Bry

Was he crazy? A vampire who was just waiting to rip out my throat, or worse was stalking me, and he wanted me to meet him in a *graveyard*? Why didn't we just meet in Josiah's coffin while we were at it? My heart was pounding in my chest. I forced myself to calm down. What Bry suggested seemed a very stupid idea indeed, but he seemed to know what he was doing. At least he had so far. We'd been meeting often in the park, planning and scheming. It seemed safe there. Maybe Bry knew something I didn't. Maybe Josiah had discovered our meeting place. When I thought about it, maybe meeting in the graveyard wasn't such a bad idea. If I was Josiah, that was the last place I'd think to look.

It was still rather light out when I reached the cemetery. Bry was nowhere to be found, of course. I didn't like being there alone. Even in the early evening light, it was spooky. Every shadow looked like something lurking, or crawling up out of a grave. Images from horror films began to invade my thoughts and I fought hard to banish them. I was scared enough already.

The graveyard wasn't very big, but I paced about nervously seeking Bry. Perhaps he was waiting on me in some remote corner hidden by mausoleums and tombstones. I couldn't find him. Terror froze my heart as a horrible thought entered my mind. What if I'd walked into some kind of trap? What if Bry was really in league with Josiah and they'd lured me here to kill me?

I knew as soon as I thought it that it was nonsense. If they were working together, I'd have been dead long ago. They'd have had any number of chances to do me in. I knew I could trust Bry, simply because I was still alive.

I stopped dead in my tracks. I swallowed hard. What if the note in my locker wasn't from Bry at all? What if it was a trick of Josiah's to get me alone and finish me? What if he was going to torture me or play sick, twisted games with me, like a cat with a mouse, until he finally ripped me to pieces? *Stop it, Graham!* I told myself. I squeezed my eyes shut and tried to force myself to calm down. I was trembling and my thoughts were racing.

"*Just chill out, Graham, and stop being so paranoid. Stop thinking so much. Everything is going to be okay,*" I thought to myself. I clutched the lemon balm I had in my pocket. It made me feel a little safer.

Where was Bry? I hoped that something bad hadn't happened to him. What if Josiah had managed to get him? I worried all the time about Josiah getting me, but he was probably after Bry too. Sure, Bry was strong and muscular, but I'd witnessed Josiah's unnatural strength. Bry might look like he could take Josiah without effort, but quite the opposite was true. No one was safe.

I felt a chill that had nothing to do with the temperature. I wrapped my arms around myself and looked about. Most of the tombstones were so old that the lettering had mostly worn away. I couldn't even begin to read some of them. What hadn't been obliterated by time was covered with moss. Cedar trees, which had probably been planted as tiny saplings, had pushed some of the tombstones over during their decades of growth. Many tombstones marked the graves of children; kids must have died in droves a hundred and more years ago. It was sad and unfair. I found a grave of a little boy that died when he was ten. He'd barely even started living. What if I'd died when I was his age? I'd have never lived the last three years of my life. I'd have missed out on so much. My life really sucked sometimes, but there was a lot of cool stuff in it too. What if

Josiah killed me now? I'd miss out on the rest of my life. I didn't want to die at thirteen. I wanted to live my life.

I jerked around; I thought I heard someone, but there was only silence and emptiness. I wished Bry would arrive. I was scared. I didn't like being alone. I gripped the lemon balm tightly. I hoped it would protect me.

I didn't feel safe. Then again, I didn't feel safe anywhere. I had begun to suspect everyone. I wondered how many vampires were already in my quiet little town and what was to be done about them. I'd focused all my thoughts on Josiah, but what of the twins and all rest? Did they all have to be destroyed too? Or was it like in the movies where all the vampires were freed when the head vampire was killed? The line between fantasy and reality had become blurred and I didn't know what to believe anymore.

I caught sight of Bry in the distance. I heaved a sigh of relief. I was thrilled to see him, even though he looked grim. Bry was my protector; so confident and strong. I knew I was safe when he was near. I wished he'd take me in his arms, hold me, and kiss me. But I could never let him know that I needed him. I couldn't take the slightest risk of offending him, and losing him. If he abandoned me, I was as good as dead.

"What took you so long?" I asked crossly. I didn't mean to sound angry, but I was frightened. "And why did we have to meet here?"

"I'm sorry. I had some preparations to make. Don't look so scared. We are on hallowed ground. Vampires cannot walk upon this earth. We're safe."

I had no idea that vampires couldn't walk in graveyards. In movies, they were often found there. I had to remind myself that I was dealing with reality, not a movie, even though my reality had become so fantastic that it seemed like a film.

"I know where Josiah lives," I said. "I saw him go into the old Maclaine house. I've seen him near there before too. I'm sure that's his home."

"Excellent! That will save us a lot of time, Graham. Good job!"

I smiled, but the next words that came from Bry's lips wiped the grin right off my face.

"We do it tonight," he said.

"Tonight?" I asked, suddenly more fearful than I'd ever been before.

"Yes, the sooner the better. We can't waste any time. Every night we wait is one more night he has to attack you, and others. Now that we know where to look, we can strike."

"But…Are you sure we have to do this? I mean…I don't think I can handle this, Bry. I just can't…I…" I'd been thinking brave thoughts about what we had to do, but that was when it was in the future. Now that it was upon me, my courage faltered.

"Graham, listen to me. I know you're scared. I know you don't want to do this. I don't want to do it either. But it must be done. He'll get you sooner or later if it isn't. He'll get a lot of others too. I know it's hard, but we've got to be brave, both of us. I'll try it alone if I must, but I need you, Graham. I don't think I can do it without you."

"I know, but I just…" Tears were flowing from my eyes. It was just too much to handle. It felt good to be needed, but why did it have to happen now, and like this? I felt like I had a purpose at last, but me? I wasn't a hero. I wasn't the kind of boy that did courageous things. I was small and puny and frightened. How was I supposed to stand up to a vampire?

"Graham, look at this," said Bry. "See what will happen if we don't stop him."

He shoved a newspaper at me. On the cover was the story of a boy who'd been found dead in the next little town. The story said he'd been attacked by some kind of big dog. There were bite marks on his neck. He had been completely drained of blood. The boy was only ten years old. I thought of the ten year old in the grave I'd seen earlier. It had happened to another boy. It wasn't fair to die so young.

"You see what he's doing. It could happen here next. It could be one of your friends. It could be you. We have to do this, Graham."

"Yes," I said, nodding my head and wiping the tears from my face. "All right, we do it and we do it tonight." I didn't feel particularly brave, but I knew what had to be done. It didn't matter that I was so scared I felt like hiding under a rock. Something had to be done, and unfortunately I was the one who had to do it.

"Go home," said Bry. "Make up some story about staying with a friend or something, then get back here just before dark. I'll be waiting. I'll have what we need to do the job. We'll take care of him, and then it will be over. By this time tomorrow you won't have to worry about having your throat ripped out in the night. Just a few more hours and it will be done. It's going to be okay, Graham."

I walked home, shaking. Oh how I wished that I could just skip over the next few hours. I wished it was already over and done with. I didn't know how I could possibly make it through the night. How could I do what I had to do? It was too horrible to even contemplate, much less actually carry through. I just knew I'd be dead before the sun rose, or worse; I'd be a vampire myself.

It seemed only seconds, and like a thousand years, before I was back in the graveyard. The sun was sinking fast. As the darkness grew, my fear increased. Why, oh why, did this happen to me?

Bry stood there waiting for me with a small gym bag. I knew what was inside. The very thought of what we were about to do made my skin crawl. I kept wanting to turn on my heel and bolt, but I knew I could not.

We walked slowly to Josiah's lair. Bry outlined the plan as we drew closer and closer. I was relieved to hear that he would do the actual act of killing Josiah. It was he who would chop off his head with the sharp hatchet he carried. I was to keep Josiah at bay with the lemon balm I carried with me. I had a whole pocket full.

"Remember, he is many times stronger than either of us. You cannot forcibly hold him down. He'll push you off as if you weighed no more than a feather. You've got to keep him down with the herb, hold it in front of his face, keeping pushing it toward him. He'll do everything he can to force you back, so beware. He'll try to frighten you. He'll lunge at you. Be prepared for anything. But remember, you've got to keep him down. If you don't, it's all over. He'll kill us both and there will be no one left to stop him."

I swallowed hard and simply nodded. I could not speak. My heart pounded so hard and fast I thought it would shoot from my chest. I had to fight to keep from hyperventilating. I was a hundred times more frightened than I'd ever been before. Even my nightmares seemed tame beside what I was feeling. It was a struggle just to keep myself from running away screaming. The only thing that kept me moving forward was the knowledge that this was the only way to save myself, and everyone else.

"When I'm ready to swing, I'll give you a nod," said Bry. "You jerk back and I'll go for his throat." Bry pulled a large hatchet out of his bag. It was heavy, with a wide blade. The newly sharpened edge gleamed. I was squeamish just looking at it.

I wished there was another way. I didn't want to kill Josiah, even though he was a monster. It might have been a very long time ago, but he'd been a boy once, just like me. He didn't ask to become what he was. He was a victim, too. It was so unfair that he had to die. All of life seemed unfair sometimes.

"When I do it, there will be blood, lots of blood. As soon as I strike turn your face away or you'll be covered in it," said Bry. I felt sick to my stomach. I felt queasy just looking at a cut, how was I going to endure this? I forced myself to keep moving. Just a few minutes more, and it would all be over.

"I can't get his head off in one blow. It'll probably take a few swings. You've got to stick in there with me, understand? You've got to keep him down. Remember, he's not human. Even after I make the first swing, he'll fight like mad. I know it's going to take all the strength of will you can muster, but you've got to keep him off me. If you don't, he'll rip me to shreds, then you'll be next."

I wished Bry would just shut up and stop talking about it. He'd told me this stuff before. Hearing it again didn't help; it only strengthened my desire to bolt from this nightmare.

The great house loomed before us. It was menacing, as if it were alive itself. I trembled. I just knew Josiah was watching us from inside, waiting to pounce on us and kill us. We were marching to certain death. Taking on a vampire was lunacy. What was I thinking? I was ready to turn and bolt, but Bry gazed at me with those sexy eyes of his and put his hand on my shoulder.

"It's going to be okay, Graham. Soon, it will all be over and you won't have to be afraid anymore."

We came to the house and found the doors and windows locked. My heart jumped as Bry tried each one. I half expected Josiah to come flying through the window at us. I was so jumpy my own shadow frightened me.

Bry wrapped his jacket around his right elbow and broke out a windowpane. I cringed at the noise it made. Bry unlocked the window and we pulled ourselves through. It was dim and creepy inside, with dark corners and a hundred places where something horrible could be hidden—it was like being inside a bad dream.

We crept around the strange house. I clutched the little bag hanging around my neck tightly. I shook from head to foot in terror. It was like the worst of my worst nightmares, and then some. My eyes were wild with terror. I had to fight to keep a scream from surging from my throat.

We crept from room to room on the first floor. There were living rooms, a dining room, a kitchen, and a lot of other rooms too, but Josiah was in none of them. The house was old beyond thinking, and yet everything was neat and tidy as if someone worked a great deal to keep it clean and neat. It wasn't at all what I was expecting. I thought the whole place would be a wreck.

We explored the entire first floor and found nothing. We found a stair leading into the basement, but neither Bry nor I were eager to go down there. In vampire movies, the coffin was always in the basement, but this wasn't a movie. I kept reminding myself of that.

We headed upstairs instead and found bedroom after bedroom. I was beginning to think that Josiah might not even be home. I feared we'd have to check out the basement after all and I wasn't looking forward to it in the least. That fear was not realized, however—we found Josiah at last. We entered yet another bedroom and there he was. I expected to find Josiah lying in a coffin, like in all the vampire stories, but he was lying stretched out on a bed, clad only in a pair of boxers. His skin was the palest I'd ever seen. He looked sweet and innocent as he lie there, but I knew he was not. Even so, his beauty drew me. This was the boy I'd sought out as a friend. This was the boy I'd had warm thoughts about. This was the boy I'd hoped would be my boyfriend. But he wasn't a boy, he was something else entirely. His looks were deceiving. He appeared innocent, but he was a killer of the worst kind.

We didn't have much time. Josiah would be rising soon. When it was a bit darker he would go out and practice his evil. Bry silently motioned me to the far side of the bed. He pulled out the hatchet and the shiny metal gleamed in the dim light. I took out the bunch of lemon balm I had stuffed in my pocket.

We leaned over Josiah—closer, closer. My hands trembled. It took every ounce of courage I had to keep from screaming. Bry raised the hatchet high in the air, holding it poised above Josiah's soft neck. I made ready to shove my lemon balm at him. I shook with terror; my eyes were blurred with tears of terror and sorrow. I hated what we were doing. I didn't want to be there. Fate had forced it upon me, however, and there was no escape.

Josiah's eyes popped open and he hissed at us, baring his long, sharp fangs. If I'd had any doubt he was a vampire, it would have been erased at that moment. I shoved the lemon balm at him even as I screamed. He shrank away from it. Bry brought the hatchet hurtling down, but could not hit his mark. Josiah knocked it away as he writhed and flailed in pain on the bed. His face was contorted with the agony caused by the herb that I held toward him. Bry straddled him and stuck with his hatchet once again, desperately trying to hit Josiah's neck. Josiah fended him off even as he fought to escape what I held mere inches from his face. Tears streamed from my eyes. I knew he had to be destroyed, but I didn't want it to be done. I didn't want Josiah harmed.

Josiah lunged straight up at me, hissing horribly, his fangs coming within inches of my neck. I screamed and fell back. Bry brought the hatchet hurtling down, but Josiah swept it away, unharmed. I heard the crack of Bry's arm as the bone within it broke from the blow. The hatchet went flying. Bry was hurled back toward me. Josiah came at us. I held my herbs out in front of me, fending him off. I knew then that we were going to die. We had failed.

Bry was behind me. I somehow found the courage to protect us both. I was our only chance at survival. I was barely holding Josiah at bay, however. He was so enraged that I feared even the herb would not keep him back for long. Perhaps the combination of the lemon balm and Bry's ring would protect us, but perhaps not. Josiah was terrifying and beautiful at the same time. I was drawn to him, even as I expected him to destroy me. At any moment, he might lunge at me and sink his teeth into my neck.

The attack came not from Josiah, however, it came from behind. My eyes widened in surprise. Pain seared my neck as the gold chain was ripped from it. Greater pain still descended upon me as sharp fangs sank into my neck. I screamed and dropped the lemon balm, falling toward the floor.

Josiah rushed forward. Bry released me and lunged for the door, but Josiah grabbed him and threw him across the room before he could escape, smashing him into the plaster wall. The wall gave under the force of the impact and plaster rained down upon us all, coating us in white. Bry jumped up as if he felt it not at all. He hissed at Josiah, baring long fangs, then hurtled himself through a window and disappeared into the night.

Josiah turned toward me. I crawled backwards toward the wall, crying hysterically. There was nowhere to go, no escape. I'd lost the herb. I was defenseless. My mind was still reeling with what I'd seen. Bry was one of them, too. Both he and Josiah had been playing with me. I'd fallen for their trap. I was as good as dead. Why had they fought? Were they fighting to determine who had the pleasure of killing me? I was in such a panic I could not think.

Josiah grabbed me and lifted me into the air without effort. My feet were dangling. I was screaming, pounding on his chest with my fists. It had no effect on him whatsoever. He lay me down on the bed as if I weighed nothing at all.

"Graham, Graham, it's okay. You're safe." He shook me. "Listen to me, Graham, you're safe. It's all right."

I would have fought him, but he held my wrists down firmly on the bed with one hand and the weight of his body was on my midsection. He was so strong I couldn't move. I was wild with terror, but he held me in place with ease.

"Go ahead! Do it! I can't stop you and you know it! Kill me! Just get it over with! Stop playing these twisted games with me. It's evil and cruel!" I screamed at him. Tears were streaming from my eyes.

"I'm not going to kill you, Graham. I'm not your enemy. Your enemy has fled. Listen to me."

I would hear none of it, but Josiah did not attack me. He did not sink his teeth into my neck. He just held me in place and looked into my eyes.

"Please," I pleaded with him, "just get it over with. Please." I cried. I couldn't handle it.

"Calm down, Graham. I need to look at where he bit you. I'm just going to look, that's all. I won't hurt you."

I was beginning to settle down. I was still terrified, but Josiah showed no signs of killing me. As I slowly regained my senses the confused events began to take shape. Bry had bit me. He had sunk his fangs into my neck. He was a vampire. He'd tricked me. But why? Why hadn't he done me in long ago? What kind of sick game were these two playing with me?

Another thought struck me that was even more bizarre. Josiah had attacked Bry and Bry had fled. They didn't act at all as if they were in league. They were both vampires. I had the bite marks to prove that Bry was one and I knew that Josiah was too. None of it made any sense. Why did Bry flee?

Josiah was carefully examining my neck. He held a piece of cloth against it.

"It doesn't look too bad, Graham," he said to me. I felt as if it was, I felt very woozy and weak. My strength was quickly leaving me. As the adrenaline from my fright wore off, I began to feel all shaky. I don't think I could have escaped from Josiah if he was nothing more than an ordinary boy.

"You're not going to kill me?" I asked. Seconds passed and still I lived. The look of concern on Josiah's features put me more at ease than his words possibly could.

"No. I'd never do that. I'm not here to harm you."

I calmed further and Josiah loosened his grip on me.

"But you're a vampire. I know you are. You killed Nate, and that boy in the next town. You've been attacking people. You attacked me. You've been stalking me."

"I am a vampire," he answered. "But not all is what it seems. I will tell you everything in time. For now, I think it is best that I take you home. Your parents will worry if they find you missing."

Josiah dressed, then lifted me from the bed without effort and carried me downstairs and out of the house. He walked through the woods, towards my home. I marveled at his strength. He carried me with more ease than I could have carried a candy bar. I was still afraid, very afraid, but I knew he was not going to harm me. If he were, he would have already done so. That made me think of something very important.

"When I was attacked in the woods, it wasn't you was it?"

"No. It was Bry. All vampires have the ability to transform into wolves. It was he who attacked you."

"But you were there, weren't you? I saw you for a moment, and I saw the wolf you become."

"Yes. I was there. I was following him. By then, I already knew what he was."

My hand flew to my neck.

"Oh no!" I said.

"What?"

"I've been bitten twice now. I'm going to be a vampire too."

"No," said Josiah

"No? But Bry said…"

"Do not trust Bry's words. It take three bites from a vampire before you become one, three bites made without taking your life."

"Then it will take one more."

"Yes, which is why you must be careful. You must take no chances, until I can take care of Bry."

Something clicked in my head just then and I understood the events of the night more clearly than before. I was also presented with new questions.

"He was using me to destroy you, but it wasn't because you are a vampire. Why does he want to kill you if you are one of his kind?"

"I'm not exactly the same," said Josiah.

My brow wrinkled in confusion.

"The explanation is a long one," said Josiah. "I will tell you all in time, but for now all you need to know is that he sought to kill me, because he knows I will kill him."

His answer did more to puzzle me than explain. So much had happened, and my head was so full, that I didn't ask more. I didn't think my mind could take it. I felt as if my wits were about to fly apart.

Josiah set me down outside my house.

"The precautions you have taken will protect you while you are inside your room, but be careful, Graham. Do not leave it without the herb you wield so well. Do not go outside by night. Do not go anywhere alone. Bry may well intend to make you into one of his own, or he may seek to kill you, now that his plan has failed. I cannot emphasize enough the danger you are in. Take no chances," he said.

I wondered how he knew about the precautions I'd taken to protect myself, but then maybe he'd seen them for himself. Maybe it was him outside my window at night, but with a different purpose than I'd feared.

"Thank you, Josiah," I said quietly, then turned and went inside. I went straight to my room and closed the door. I lay on my bed. I was so exhausted that I fell instantly into a deep sleep.

CHAPTER 11

Josiah's Other Life

When I awakened the next morning, I could not believe that what had happened the night before was real. I would have thought it all a dream, but the bite marks on my neck were clear evidence that the events of the night before were not a product of my imagination. My head was spinning with it all.

I didn't see Josiah until lunchtime, but as I came out of line with my tray, there he was, sitting all alone. I mourned the time I'd lost with him and was pained by his loneliness, which I had helped to increase by avoiding him. I walked straight to him and stood before him.

"I'm sorry for…everything," I said. My words definitely didn't cover what needed said.

"It's quite all right," said Josiah. "Have a seat."

I smiled and sat down across from him, as I had so often before. When I'd discovered that Josiah was a vampire, I never thought things would be the same again. I was glad to be wrong. I'd missed him.

"You had good reason to fear me," said Josiah. "You acted reasonably, bravely even. You did not know you had been misled."

"But I…I tried to kill you," I said in a whisper.

"Had I been what you thought, you would have been right to do so. You would have been doing me, and everyone else, a favor."

Josiah was what I thought, a vampire, but it was clear that the situation was far more complex than it seemed. He was a vampire, but he was not a killer. It wasn't him who had killed Nate and that other boy. I believed that now. It wasn't him who had bitten the twins, at least I didn't think so.

We did not talk more about it because we feared someone would overhear. We agreed to meet right after school. I had many questions and Josiah had a lot of explaining to do.

I was thinking a lot about Josiah, in between classes and in study hall. The excitement of having him as a friend had returned. Our friendship was uncertain, because of what he was, but I still had hopes for it. My heart had hopes of its own. I felt something for Josiah more than friendship. Part of what had made everything so difficult with Josiah was the way I felt about him. I cared for him; warm thoughts about him had filled my heart. When I'd found out he was a vampire, it had been twice as hard because it dashed my hopes. Now, that hope was returning. I found myself daydreaming about holding Josiah's hand and about him holding me in his arms. I knew I was getting well ahead of myself, but my heart could not be silenced. And to think I'd nearly helped Bry destroy Josiah. I shuddered at the thought. Never in my life I was I more glad to have failed.

※　　　　　※　　　　　※

I gazed at Josiah as we walked away from school.

"You're really a vampire," I said. "I just can't believe it."

"I'd think you'd be able to believe it after everything that has happened," said Josiah.

"Well, I do believe it, it's just hard to believe…you know? I mean vampires are myths, or I always thought they were."

"All myths are based in fact," said Josiah. "The city of Troy was mythical until someone discovered it was really there. King Arthur, Robin Hood, and many others were once thought to be myths too. So it is with vampires, and many other things."

Josiah seemed very wise for his years. He was a lot smarter than any fifteen-year-old boy I knew. I looked at him intently, truly realizing for the first time that he wasn't fifteen at all.

"How old are you?" I asked him. "How old are you *really*?"

"Hmm, I'm not sure. I haven't thought about that for a long time. Birthday's become rather meaningless after a point. Let's see." Josiah thought for several long moments before he answered. The pause made his words seem all the more dramatic. "Yes. I remember now. I was born in England in the year 1064."

"But that would make you well over nine hundred years old!" I said.

My mouth dropped open and I gaped at him. Josiah was hundreds and hundreds of years old and yet he looked like a fifteen-year-old boy. In many ways he acted like one too. I wondered how that was possible after nearly a thousand years.

"Quite true."

"You still seem fifteen to me," I said. Josiah smiled.

"My body is fifteen, and will always be. As for the rest of me, well, we are all as old or young as we think. Despite the years I've lived, I still think of myself as fifteen, I still feel that age, and so that's the age I am. I've always lived my life as a fifteen year old. I couldn't live it as someone older if I wanted to, just look at me."

I saw what he meant. He might have hundreds of years of experiences and knowledge, but everyone would always see him as a boy. I knew I would.

My mind was bursting with questions. It was hard to decide which to ask first. One question rose above the rest, however.

"How did you become a vampire, Josiah?"

He looked at me as if deciding whether he would tell me or not, then began to speak.

"I am not a full vampire, and the reason for that has to do with how I was made. There are some differences between a full vampire and me, which is why I fought to save you, rather than destroy you."

"Differences?" I asked, interrupting him.

"Yes, most of them are merely a matter of degree, and in many ways I am exactly the same, but there is one way in which I differ greatly."

"And that is?"

"I do not need to feed on the blood of others. I can, but I have other ways to survive. I must draw off the life of those around me in order to live without pain, but I can do so without causing harm. I do not need blood. I can take what I need in other ways."

"How?" I asked, most curious.

"All vampires are able to feed upon emotions. Any emotion will do, but fear is one of the most powerful. It is much easier to induce great fear, instead of happiness or love, especially if one is a creature such as a vampire. Vampires seek to create intense fear in their victims. They feed upon it as much as they do the blood. Full vampires must have the blood, however, while I do not need it. I can exist solely on what I draw from the emotion.

"I've learned how to take what I need without doing harm to my victims. I could drain someone of their life-force and kill them as if I had sucked out all their blood, but if I take only a little, they don't even notice it's been done. I draw off a little of what I need from everyone I pass and need not take much from any. It makes it possible for me to exist, without the need to kill."

I looked at him as if I didn't believe him. I wasn't sure I did. I didn't think he was lying, but it was just too unbelievable to swallow.

"I'll show you," he said. "Do not be afraid. I won't harm you, I'll only draw enough of your energy for you to feel it without doubt."

I stood there looking at him. I couldn't tell he was doing anything, then slowly I began to feel weaker. I could feel my very life began to flow out and I knew he was drawing it from me. I swayed, then the feeling abruptly stopped.

"I've felt that before!" I said. "Not when I was with you, but when I was with Bry. Sometimes I felt emotionally drained, as if my life were oozing out of me. Then last night, as he bit me, I felt it again, only it was so powerful I thought I'd die."

"You are very perceptive," said Josiah. "I should have expected that, however. You are not an ordinary boy. Bry has been very clever. He's concealed himself well. He's been wise enough to take great care when he feeds. You felt it so strongly last night because he made no effort to conceal what he was doing. He was attempting to take all he could from you. He was attempting to kill you. Fortunately, he did not have enough time.

I swallowed hard. I knew I'd come very close to death.

"Wait!" I said, throwing my arm across Josiah's chest. We were about to step into the graveyard. We'd been so busy talking he hadn't even noticed.

"What is it?"

I indicated the graveyard. Josiah did not comprehend.

"You can't go in there."

"I don't see any reason why not."

"But Bry said…Duh!"

"What?"

"Bry told me we were safe from you when we met in the graveyard last night, because vampires couldn't come onto hallowed ground. He had to be lying, though, because he's a vampire himself."

"Yes. He was lying. I assure you I'll be quite safe."

We stepped into the graveyard and Josiah showed no ill effects. We made our way to a stone bench and sat there under the shade of an ancient cedar.

"I wonder what else he lied to me about," I said.

"Perhaps a great deal. I'd seek out other sources of information on vampires if I were you."

Josiah was quite right. I was glad I had other sources. The greatest of them all was sitting before me—a real vampire. I thought about what Josiah had said about drawing life from others. Something dawned on me.

"You go to school because there's lots of people there, don't you? That way you can take a little from many and they don't even know it."

"You're right, to an extent. I seek out large crowds so that I may feed without bringing harm to any. I could easily do that by walking through a mall or attending a ballgame, however. The real reason I attend school is so that I can live some part of a normal life. Immortality is not all it's cracked up to be."

I understood. Josiah was lonely. Being around all those young people eased the pain of that, somewhat. I wondered why he didn't involve himself more, however, instead of keeping himself apart. Was it the fear of being found out for what he was? Or was there more? I didn't have time to think about it, for Josiah spoke again.

"To go on with my story. I was fifteen when it happened—really fifteen. I was working late in the fields. My parents were poor serfs on a large estate northeast of what is now London and eked out a marginal living for themselves, my brother, and me. It was a good life in many ways, but not so in others. There was never enough food. I was always hungry. What we did have to eat was seldom what I wanted, although when you are starving, you are grateful for anything you can get.

"I was pulling weeds out of our crops by hand, as I had been the entire day. It had grown dark, but still I worked. My father worked himself to exhaustion, so I did what I could to help him. My father was a good man."

Josiah looked very sad. I imagined that he missed his family very much. I couldn't even imagine how homesick he must be for them, after more than nine hundred years.

"In the moonlight I saw a young woman walking along the road that bordered the field I was working in. She saw me and came in my direction. I remember being surprised at that because she was wearing very fine clothes and I found it odd that such a woman would tromp through the dirt and mud when there was nothing of interest in our field. There was something there that captured her interest, however—me.

"As she drew close I noted that she was older than me, around twenty-one or so. She was very beautiful. I was suspicious of her, of course. She was quite out of place in our field. She spoke kindly to me and offered me an apple, which I gladly took. My stomach was growling with hunger and an apple was something I'd rarely seen before.

"As I devoured it she drew closer. She took my chin in her hand and told me what an attractive boy I was. I was very naïve at the time, even ignorant. I was a peasant and nothing more. She pulled me to her and my only thought was that I'd get her fine clothes dirty. She smelled very clean and nice. I, of course, had not bathed in weeks and no doubt reeked. She didn't seem to mind, however. She pulled me close and nuzzled my neck. I didn't' even know it at the time, but she sank her teeth into me and fed on my blood. I didn't feel it. It didn't hurt. She just held me and petted my hair for several moments while she sucked my blood.

"She raised her face from my neck, but still stood quite close. I remember the look of hunger in her eyes as she gazed at me, but I gave it little heed. I was concentrating on her words. She told me about all the things there were to eat at her home. I listened to her describing roast pig and deer, sweet breads and cooked vegetables, and even wonderful deserts. It seemed like a fairy story to me. She held me spellbound with her tales of food.

"She asked me to meet her the next evening in the nearby village. There she would take me to her home and I could have whatever I wanted to eat. When the evening was done, I could even bring all I could carry back to my family. I was to tell no one, however. To this I quickly agreed.

"After she left all I could think of was that I would not be hungry the next night and that my family would not be either. I could just image their faces when I returned, triumphant, loaded down with good things to eat. As I trudged back to the hovel that was my home, I did begin to wonder why she was doing all this for me. My father had warned me of strangers, but his warnings held little power when my mind was filled with thoughts of food. You may think I was foolish, and indeed I was, but when you are hungry, very, very hungry, thoughts of a feast are a temptation that cannot be resisted.

"I said nothing to my parents. If I had done so, they would have warned me not to meet the stranger and my life would have been quite different. People were far more aware of such things as vampires then. My father might even have figured out the true nature of the beautiful young stranger who was luring me away. I was a naïve and foolish boy and could think of nothing more than all the food I'd have to eat, so I said nothing, and doomed myself to an eternal life.

"I had dreams that night of a great feast and there was little else that I could think of on waking. As I toiled in the fields all day, I just kept thinking about the stranger and her fine clothes and what she'd offered me. I even fantasized that she'd ask me to live with her and that I'd have nice clothes to wear and never be hungry again.

"That day seemed to last forever, but finally the night came. I sneaked away and walked the three miles to the little village. It was little more than a cluster of homes with a sagging inn, but it seemed quite a big place to me. The stranger was there waiting on me. I didn't know her name and I never learned it, but she was beautiful, more beautiful than any girl or woman I'd ever seen. She said nothing to me, but led me away from the village, straight toward the castle of the lord.

"The feudal lord controlled all and was rather like a king on a smaller scale. My world was a small one. I'd never been more than ten miles from my home, so to me he was a king. I shook with fear as we neared the huge stone castle. I'd seen it only from a distance. Close up it was bigger than anything I'd ever imagined. I closed my eyes as we crossed over the drawbridge and walked through the immense gates. It was too much for me to take in.

"The stranger led me to her private apartment and it was luxurious beyond anything I'd ever imagined. It was beyond my dreams. There were tapestries on the walls and skins of bear and other wild creatures on the floor. What drew my attention the most was the table heavily laden with food. The stranger had not lied to me about all there was to eat there.

"She seated me at the table and told me to eat whatever I wanted. She left me alone and I devoured what was before me. There was roast pig and duck, puddings, sauces, and many things that I had never seen and could not name. Never before in my life had I been able to sit down and eat all I wanted. I was sure that I was in a dream, but even if I was I intended to gorge myself. I ate and ate until I could eat no more. I was happy and content. There was still an entire feast left, but I was far too full to take a single bite more.

"The stranger returned. She smiled at me, but there was something in her smile that made me uncomfortable. I suddenly felt like a rabbit staring into the eyes of a hawk. A fear rose in me, and yet I felt that I was being ungrateful for what she had given me. I trembled as she ran her fingertips across my face and told me what a pretty boy I was. I liked the things she was saying to me and believed that I was beginning to understand her interest in me. I was mistaken, however.

"She moved her face toward my neck as she had the night before, but this time I jerked back in fear. Something within me told me I was in great danger. That's when I saw her fangs. That's when I realized what she was.

"Everything happened so fast then that it was all a blur. She attacked me, sinking her teeth deep into my neck. It was not painless as it had been previously. I could feel her sucking the living blood from my body. I thought she would drain me, but she stopped.

"I did not know it then, but she intended to make me into a creature like herself. She had bitten me twice and once more would seal my fate. She herself told me her plans now that she was revealed. She intended for me to live through eternity with her as her lover.

"She leaned in and sank her teeth into my neck yet again. I was not witless, however. At that same moment she lowered herself upon me, I snatched a large knife out of a roast goose and slashed at her with it. I was not educated. I was only an ignorant serf, but I knew as everyone did that the only way to stop a vampire was to take off its head.

"I severed her neck at the very moment her teeth sank into me, nearly cutting my own throat in the process. I killed her at the very moment she began to feed on my blood. She crashed to the floor and I bolted, not even stopping to gather any of the feast that was there before me. I raced from the castle and ran all the way home, my neck throbbing in pain."

"Didn't her head have to be burned, to keep her from coming back?" I asked.

"That is the traditional way in which vampires are killed," said Josiah. "They can be brought back if their head is not destroyed, if there is someone to perform the incantation. Luckily for me, no one sought to bring her back from the grave. Perhaps even others suspected her for what she was and disposed of her head it when it was discovered she was slain.

"I never told my parents what had happened, nor my brother. I was able to hide the bite marks on my neck until they healed. Things went on as they always had and I thought that the events of that night were over and done with, as horrible as they were. Only with the passing of time did I realize what had happened to me.

"A year passed, then two and I did not change. I did not grow taller, nor broader. My younger brother surpassed me in height, although I'd always been the taller. Even though my brother was a year younger than I, he matured while I did not. He grew whiskers on his face, while my features remained clean.

"I turned eighteen and still I appeared not to have aged a day. I seemed not to change at all. I had become more sensitive to light, but I didn't think about that much. It didn't seem significant at the time. I did not grow in stature, but I did grow in strength. I had always been a strong boy from all the manual labor I performed, but slowly my physical strength increased. It did so at a gradual rate, however, a quicker pace than was normal, but I was ignorant of that.

"By the time I turned twenty-one, I knew that something was definitely wrong. I had not aged a day in the last six years. My parents and brother knew that something was amiss too. We did not discuss it, but everyone knew it. My brother had grown into a man, while I was still a boy. It was in that year, however, that I figured out what had happened to me.

"There were many small wars at that time. One feudal lord was forever attacking another. My brother and I were summoned to fight for our lord as the army of a neighboring lord neared. It was our duty as his serfs.

"It was a battle of only some seventy or eighty men, but the fighting was fierce. There were only some twenty of us standing against a much larger force. I watched as my brother was pierced through the throat with an arrow. He fell dead. In a rage I attacked our enemies. It was foolish. I attacked a knight with nothing more than a sharpened stick. He pierced my heart with his broadsword, driving it straight through my body. I fell to the ground in pain, but did not die. I could not die.

"Our enemies overran the field and set fire to the village and the outlying farms. All was destroyed. I lay on the ground for some time, knowing that I should be dead, realizing for the first time what I had become. I examined my flesh through the tears in my clothing and found that I had already healed. My mind raced back to the night with the stranger. At that moment I knew I was a vampire."

"And your parents?" I asked. "What became of them?"

"Killed. I returned to my home to find it gone, burned. My parents lay dead near it. It was the same everywhere. The serfs could not defend themselves against the army that attacked, small as it was. Only those within the castle walls survived. The rich weathered the attack, while the poor died.

"I buried my parents and little brother, then left that place forever. There was nothing for me there. All that I had known was destroyed. Even I had changed into something I did not understand. I began to wander the world, to live in one place for a time, then move on before anyone grew wise to the fact that I did not age."

"Um, I still don't understand why you don't need to drink blood," I said as we sat on the cool stone bench.

"Because the creature that made me was killed at the very moment of my making, something did not pass into me that should have, some part of my transformation was not complete. Some little part of me remained human. Whatever went wrong freed me from the need to feed on blood. Instead, I could survive solely on the energy of those around me. It was for that reason that it took me so long to realize what I had become. I ate as I always had and thought that nothing had changed. I did not know, however, that I was drawing energy from those around me, from my very own family. Our life was hard and exhausting, so it was never suspected."

Josiah grew quiet. There was tons more I wanted to know, but I think talking about it kind of made him sad. I fought the urge to ask him some more of the questions that were on my mind. We had plenty of time. I didn't have to learn everything all at once.

"Josiah," I said, "I'm really glad that you aren't what I thought you were. Well, you are a vampire, but I mean I'm glad you aren't the kind that hurts people. Before I got the wrong idea about you, I think we were becoming friends. I liked that and I hope we can pick up where we left off." There was more I wanted to say. I wished to speak of my hopes that we would become more than friends, but I held my tongue.

Josiah looked even sadder than before.

"I don't know if that's such a good idea," he said. His words hit me like a slap in the face.

"Why? Don't you like me?" I asked.

"I like you very much," said Josiah. "It's just…dangerous."

"Dangerous? Why would it be dangerous? You said yourself you don't drink blood. What do I have to fear from you? I don't even mind if you feed on my energy. I wouldn't mind that at all."

"Not dangerous for you," said Josiah. "Dangerous for me." His sadness deepened. I could read it clearly on his handsome features.

"Huh? I don't understand."

"You will change. I will not. You will grow old and someday die. I won't. I'll be fifteen forever. Do you have any idea what that's like? I always hear people say they want to live forever, but it's a curse. Can you imagine having to see everyone you care about die? Every friend, everyone you love? I've made lots of friends in my life, and I've lived to see every single one of them die. It doesn't matter how young they are when I meet them, sooner or later, they grow old and I'm alone again."

"I'd never thought of that."

"There's no reason you should have. You are mortal. Some friends you make will outlive you, some will not, but you don't have to live knowing that every single friend you make will die before you do. I have to live with that. It's the curse of immortality. You don't know what it's like, making a friend and watching him die, then making another friend and watching him die too. After a while it hurts so much that you just don't want anyone to grow close, because you know they'll just die and leave you alone again."

"I'm so sorry," I said. I felt as if I really understood, as if I could feel his pain.

"It hurts," said Josiah. "Always being alone. It takes whatever joy there is out of everything."

"So that's why you didn't let anyone get close to you at school, except me."

"Yes, that's why."

"What made me different? Why did you let me get close?"

"You were more persistent than anyone else for one thing. You just wouldn't go away." I smiled at that. "And you remind me of someone—someone who was very special to me."

I could tell Josiah was on the verge of tears.

"If you don't want to tell me…"

"No," he said, "I'd like to tell you about him. He meant so much to me. I loved him so much." Josiah actually did cry for a few moments, then he went on. "His name was Zachary. I met him in a little town in Virginia about…" I could tell Josiah was calculating the years that had passed. "Could it be so long? It was about two hundred years ago, not long after the revolutionary war. Even then I kept others at arm's length, but he didn't let that stop him. He was annoyingly persistent, just like you."

I smiled.

"He wouldn't go away and I found myself liking him. We became good friends. As time passed, we became best friends. Oh, he was so much fun! The things we used to do. The trouble we used to get into!" Josiah actually laughed and I found myself smiling at him as he shared his memories.

"We remained friends for more than two years and I knew that soon it was time to go. By then the fact that I wasn't aging was becoming obvious. Zac was fifteen when we met and in two years he'd shot up and was more man than boy. I was unchanged and I knew it would soon become something I could not hide. I didn't want to go, however. I couldn't bear the thought of leaving him. I'd never had such a good friend before.

"Zachary found me sitting by a stream, crying. I told him I had to leave him soon. He begged me not to. I wanted to stay more than anything, but I knew those around me would grow suspicious soon and I would be in danger. I considered staying anyway and facing the danger, even though I knew I'd eventually be found out, that eventually they'd cut off my head.

"I cried more than ever and Zachary begged me to tell him what was wrong. My tears bothered him so that he cried too. I knew then how very much he loved me. For the very first time in all my life I told someone what I was. I told Zachary I was a vampire. All the color drained from his face and he looked shocked, but I knew that he believed me. I could tell from the look on his face that all the pieces had fallen into place for him, just as they did for you.

"After I revealed my horrible secret I expected his love to turn to hate, but he hugged me and told me he didn't care what I was, that he knew I was good and kind, and that I would forever be his best friend.

"My heart was troubled, however. I told Zachary how I could not stay. To my utter delight he asked to come with me. He told me he'd follow wherever I went. He didn't care where we were, as long as we could be together.

"For the first time in my life, I was not alone. We traveled all over the world, seeing so many wonderful things. Money was never a problem. One advantage of living forever is that you have a lot of time to accumulate wealth. By then I already had a fortune so vast it would have taken centuries to spend. We had no need to work, or do anything that we didn't want to do. We spent our lives enjoying ourselves. It was the best time of my life and what I liked best of all was that Zachary was by my side."

I began to wonder something about Josiah as he spoke of Zachary with such great love. He spoke of him not as one does a friend, but as one speaks of a lover. It was more in his expression than anything else, but his expression changed the meaning of his words. I began to hope that maybe, just maybe, Josiah was like me.

"The years passed and although they did not touch me, they did touch Zachary. When we first met we were both fifteen, but soon he was twenty-five and I had not aged a day. Ten years later and he was thirty-five, and I was still fifteen. It wasn't many years before most people thought I was Zachary's son, and we often posed as father and son to fool the ignorant. The years kept passing, however, and they took their toll.

"Before we knew it, others took me for Zachary's grandson. He had grown old, but I was still a boy of fifteen. He asked me often if I wanted to leave him and find someone younger, but I always told him that I could have no better friend and that I never wanted to leave his side, and I always meant it.

"Time passed quickly and Zachary grew ill. We could no longer travel. We'd spent nearly sixty years together, but I knew our time was at its end. One night as he lie sleeping, his breath grew shallow. I sat on the edge of the bed and looked down at him. I drew him to me and wrapped my arms around him. I held him as he took his last breaths. I cried for what seemed like forever. I couldn't believe he was gone. When he died he was seventy-one, and I was still fifteen. We'd been friends for nearly sixty years."

Tears were running from my eyes and from Josiah's. He looked at me and smiled through his tears.

"I've never told anyone about that," said Josiah. He looked at me closely. "You look so much like Zachary. You could be his twin."

I felt a little self-conscious, and a little guilty that my very looks probably brought back memories that were painful for Josiah. I knew that the memories were pleasant for him too, but it had been a long time since he'd been with Zachary. I couldn't imagine the pain of that.

"After Zachary died, I closed myself off from the world. Oh, I still moved about in it, but I let no one close. I wanted to have friends desperately. I knew I had so much to share with them, but I knew I'd lose them in the end, just like I'd lost Zac, just like I'd lost them all. The pain of that was too much to bear. The friendship and good times weren't worth it. The more I cared about someone, the more it hurt when I inevitably lost them."

I looked at Josiah with tears in my eyes. I'd never imagined that eternal life could be so painful. The very act of having fun with someone was a reminder that they'd soon be gone.

"Um…can't you just let yourself die, Josiah?" I asked. "If it's so very painful to live, can't you just not feed and let yourself die? I don't want you to do it, but I'm wondering…"

"Unfortunately, that is not an option. I considered that very thing myself. I researched the possibility. I discovered that vampires who do not feed experience unbearable pain, but do not die. I even thought that since I was not a normal vampire, that I might be able to end my own life that way, but I was wrong. I tried it. I isolated myself completely and fed not at all. At first it was like the feeling of being hungry I remembered from my life as a real boy, but then the pain grew worse. It became excruciating. It felt as if I were starving, and as if every part of my body were withering in flames. I could not bear it for long and went out into the night to feed. I was so hungry and in such pain that I had to be very cautious not to kill those I fed upon. I managed it by going into a crowd and drawing only some of what I needed from each."

"That must have been horrible," I said.

"It was like being tortured." Josiah paused. He looked as if he was in pain. "I know you probably have a lot of questions, but can we talk of something else for a while, something besides me being a vampire?"

"Yes, yes of course," I told him. I looked at him for a moment thoughtfully. "Do you like to run?"

"I love to run."

"Would you like to, go for a long run? I love to just run and run sometimes, but I've never had anyone to go with me. No one can keep up." I laughed.

"Then let's do it," said Josiah, his eyes sparkling.

We stood and started running slowly. Soon our legs had carried us out of town and along country roads. We passed the old amusement park and still we ran on. I picked up the pace and Josiah ran beside me. I loved feeling the wind flying through my hair. I loved feeling my own heart beat and the muscles in my legs tensing and flexing. I felt very in touch with myself when I ran. I ran often in fear, which I did not enjoy at all, but I also ran because I loved to do it, and because I was good at it.

I'd never had anyone who could run with me. Kelly had tried, but couldn't begin to keep pace with me. I looked at Josiah as we ran side by side. He did it without effort. While my breath came fast, his was perfectly normal. He ran with complete ease. I wondered what it must be like to have that kind of strength and ability. I'd always been on the puny side and I wondered what it must be like to be so very strong.

I soon forgot my thoughts and just enjoyed running with Josiah. I enjoyed his company, and his friendship. I knew he was not what he appeared to be, but I still thought of him as just another boy. Josiah looked at me and smiled. I think he knew that is how I thought of him, and I think he liked it.

Josiah was a boy I could fall in love with. I'd thought often of finding a friend, and it seemed I had. I had not given much thought to a boyfriend, mainly because I thought it was so impossible, but looking at Josiah running by my side, I did think about it. He would be the coolest boyfriend ever. So much was happening so fast that I thought it wise to not dwell upon it. I was still getting my bearings with all the recent changes in my life. I needed to take one thing at a time.

I halted after we'd run miles, nearly gasping for breath. Josiah looked as though he'd merely been out for a short walk.

"I...have to...go to...work," I said between breaths.

"I'll see you safely there," said Josiah. His words reminded me that I was still in danger. Bry was no doubt after me. I couldn't help but be happy, however. No one would ever know how badly I'd needed a friend, and I had him at last. I just hoped that he wouldn't leave me. I wanted him to be a part of my life always. I wanted it desperately, but I knew Josiah might draw away from me for fear of the pain of someday losing me. Somehow, I had to keep that from happening.

Josiah and I ran to the lane that led to Mr. Diggory's house. Josiah looked thoughtful as we parted, but only warned me to be careful on my way home. I had the feeling that I wouldn't be alone when I left Basil's for the evening. I had the feeling I'd be guarded by a wolf with bright blue eyes.

CHAPTER 12

❁

A Changed Life

*B*asil was as cheerful as ever as I entered the house, as were his little dogs. The pot was simmering away on the stove as always and it seemed that nothing had changed. There was a large pile of packages on the table that Basil asked me to open and put away. Each was filled with one herb or another. I wondered why he didn't have me fetch the parcels myself, but I asked no questions. I was paid well and enjoyed all that I did.

I thought about Josiah a lot as I worked. I felt something for him—inside. I'd never experienced it before, but I thought I knew what it was. I was falling in love with him. I wondered what he would think about that. I wondered if I was right about him and Zachary, or if it was just my imagination. Even if I was wrong, even if Josiah wasn't like me, maybe he'd still understand. Being a young, gay boy was a lot like being a vampire. We both had to hide our true natures. We both had to pretend to be something we were not. We both lived in constant danger. And in both our cases, there was more to us than anyone would ever guess. For the first time in my life, I considered telling someone the truth about me. Perhaps it was time to be truthful about my feelings for Josiah as well. I knew his secret. Maybe it was time he learned mine.

Of course, I wasn't sure I was gay. I'd been uncertain of that for a long time. It wasn't that I was gay and was just afraid to admit it either. I was confused. Things weren't clear-cut and black and white. The evidence was mounting, but still there was doubt. My feelings for Josiah made me pretty sure, more sure than I'd ever been. For the first time ever, I began to think of myself as most likely gay. For the first time ever, I began to refer to myself as a gay boy. I still wasn't entirely certain, but I was pretty sure.

The two hours or so I spent at Basil's that evening were pleasant and passed quickly. It always seemed as if it were time to go almost as soon as I arrived. The shadows were lengthening as I departed and I hurried along home. I'd forgotten my fears while I was with Mr. Diggory, but they came back full force once I'd gone.

My life seemed almost too fantastic to believe. If I told anyone I needed to hurry home for fear of vampires they'd probably have locked me up somewhere, and yet it was true. I didn't like the threat of maiming and death hanging over my head, but my life was definitely a lot more interesting than it had ever been in the past.

🍁   🍁   🍁

Kelly was always asking questions about Josiah, questions I was often reluctant to answer. I decided that the time had come to let her get her own answers. As we were leaving the line at lunch, I invited her to join me and sit with Josiah.

As we neared, I thought that maybe I should have asked him first, but he didn't seem to mind Kelly's presence. I'd told him a bit about her before and he knew she was one of my few friends, my only friend really. Kelly's eyes were on Josiah almost all the time. I knew she had a bit of a crush on him, well more than a bit. It probably wasn't wise to encourage that, especially not if what I suspected was true. If Josiah wasn't interested in girls, then Kelly's crush sure couldn't go anywhere. I hoped that was the case. I didn't really need to worry either way. If he did like girls, then he wouldn't be interested in me as anything more than a friend. If he liked boys, then I didn't have to worry about being in competition with Kelly. I guess the only problem would be that he might like both. I didn't let myself think about it too much. It was a whole new line of thought for me anyway. I hadn't been thinking, in *that* way, about anyone until recently, not until Josiah came along.

I'd told Kelly that Josiah had been harassing me, back when I thought he was dangerous. After I'd learned the truth, I'd managed to explain that it was all a big misunderstanding, without telling her anything I didn't want her to know. Kelly believed me. She always believed me. I felt very guilty for having lied in the first place, but I'd done it with good reason.

We ate and laughed and talked. It was good to see Josiah laugh. Despite his incredible abilities, I felt sorry for him. I couldn't imagine how painful it must be to be so very alone. I knew that he must always feel different from everyone else—an outsider. Josiah was my friend, so I worked very hard to make him feel that he belonged. It seemed to be working. Sitting there, he looked like any other fifteen-year-old boy. It was the first time ever than he seemed to really fit in.

Bry passed as we sat there and looked at us in hatred and fear. Well, he looked at Josiah in hatred and fear. I knew he didn't fear me. When he looked at me, Bry just looked hungry. I felt like a fool for being so taken in by him. I couldn't believe he'd actually been able to manipulate me into helping him try to destroy Josiah. What if we'd succeeded? I'd have killed my best friend, and would have been killed myself, or turned into a horrible creature like Bry, that fed on the pain and blood of others. I shuddered just thinking about it.

I forced it out of my mind. It was difficult to carry on a normal conversation while I was thinking such thoughts. It was hard not to think them, however. I'd come to the brink of disaster and only Josiah had pulled me back.

I gazed at Josiah as he sat there across from me. Was there really any doubt about my feelings for him? Whenever I was near him, I felt drawn to him and got this weird, but not unpleasant feeling in my chest. My arms ached to hold him. As I sat there, I pictured holding Josiah close and pressing my lips to his…My last doubts were erased. Yes, I was a gay boy. My feelings for Josiah made that clear. I was drawn to him and it wasn't just the desire for a friend. I loved him. My body responded to him. I yearned for him.

I realized I was dreamily staring at Josiah. He didn't seem to notice and that was a relief. I turned my head to the side and my eyes met those of Kelly. Her gaze was level and she smiled slightly. I swallowed hard and my eyes grew a bit wider. We sat there and looked at each other. In my heart I could feel it; she *knew.*

I grew uncomfortable and wolfed down the last of my banana pudding. I beat a hasty retreat, my face reddening with embarrassment.

I avoided Kelly after lunch, but she caught up with me just after school. I was stuffing books in my locker, hoping to get away without talking to her, but there she was, heading my way. There was no time to escape. I felt like a cornered beast. My eyes darted nervously about as she bore down upon me. I felt panic rising in my gut.

"Will you walk me home, Graham?" she asked.

I swallowed hard as I had at lunch.

"I…I, um…"

"We need to talk, Graham." Kelly leaned in closely and whispered to me, smiling, "It's going to be okay, Graham. I'm happy for you."

I felt like my face just might be on fire, but I nodded my head and we strolled out of the school. Neither of us said a word for the longest time. I just couldn't make any words come out, and besides, there were too many kids around. When at last we were alone, Kelly spoke.

"You *really* like Josiah, don't you, Graham?"

"Yeah," I admitted, "he's a cool guy. We're friends." My chest swelled with those words. I felt proud to have such a friend.

"Yes, but it's more than that, isn't it?" Kelly gave me a sideways glance. I didn't answer. I ducked my head a little, embarrassed.

"Graham, do you…do you like boys?"

I jerked my head up. I felt panicky and fearful.

"It's okay if you do, Graham. It doesn't matter to me whether you like girls or boys. I just want you to be happy."

"Am I…like, obvious?" I asked, finally. "Do I seem…gay?"

"No, you don't seem gay. It's just that you've never been interested in girls. Mainly, it's the way you look at Josiah—with love in your eyes."

I turned my head to Kelly and bit my lip. I felt joy and sadness at the same moment. I wanted to both laugh and cry.

"I *do* love him," I said, barely above a whisper. I ducked my head again.

Kelly stopped and took my face in her hands.

"Don't be embarrassed, Graham. I think it's wonderful. I'm so happy that you've found someone."

"Well, I don't know if he's interested in me, especially in…*that* way," I said.

"I think he might be," said Kelly, pinching my cheek.

"Really?"

"Well, I can't be sure, but I've just got this feeling."

"Oh, how I wish he was!" I said. I couldn't believe I was talking so openly about how I felt about another boy.

"There's one way to find out."

"How?"

"Ask him."

"I couldn't do that!"

"Then how are you ever gonna know?"

"I don't know, but I can't just *ask*. What if he says 'no', or gets mad or somethin'? Guys can get pretty bent out of shape over somethin' like that."

"I'd give it some serious thought if I were you," said Kelly.

I nodded. We kept walking and talking and the words came easier. Kelly's total acceptance of me made it easier to talk about things I never thought I'd discuss with anyone. She made me feel loved and secure. Not only that, she loved the *real* me, not the one that everyone else saw. Kelly gave me hope and courage, maybe someday I could tell Josiah how I felt about him.

I thought about what she'd said after I dropped her off at her house. I thought about it all evening and night. I thought about it so much I thought my head might explode. I wanted to tell Josiah what was in my heart—I just didn't know if I'd ever have the courage.

❦   ❦   ❦

Despite the fear hanging over my head, the next days were the most wonderful in my life. I spent a great deal of time with Josiah and we had a marvelous time. He didn't have to hide what he was around me and I think he enjoyed that a great deal. I enjoyed having another boy for a friend. For the first time in my life I had someone to do guy stuff with. Kelly was great, but she wasn't much interested in wrestling, or climbing trees, or playing basketball, or video games, or just doing something simple like skipping rocks across a pond. Josiah was into all that stuff. I was beginning to think of us as Tom and Huck again.

I don't know if two friends ever enjoyed each other as much as Josiah and I did. I'd never had a friend like him and he hadn't had one in a very, very long time either. I'd gone without a boy as my friend my entire life, but Josiah had gone without one far, far longer than that. I couldn't imagine lacking such friendship for all those years.

I was amazed at some of Josiah's abilities. One day after school, we explored the weight room where all the football jocks worked out. We saw a really muscular boy doing the bench press with 200 pounds. I could tell it was a strain for him, but he lifted it ten times in a row. We watched as his muscles bulged with the effort. He looked so *fine*. Just looking at his muscles made me breathe a little harder. After he left, and we were alone in the room, I had Josiah show me how much weight he could lift. To my amazement, he moved the weight all the way up to the maximum of 500 pounds. He lie down on the bench and lifted it with ease. He did it ten times, then went on. He didn't look anywhere near as built as that football player, but he was lifting twice the weight and it looked like he could go on forever.

When we were playing catch, I got an idea. I got an old ball and asked Josiah to throw it as far as he could. After what he'd done in the weight room, I just had to see how far he could throw. I watched as he whipped the ball into the air. It just kept arcing through the air until it grew so small I couldn't see it anymore. Josiah was like Superman or something.

"It must be hard to hide what you can do," I said.

"Yeah, it really is," said Josiah, grinning. "One advantage of living forever is that there's plenty of time to practice. You wouldn't believe how many times I've played football, and soccer, and baseball, and everything else. Sometimes it's hard to hold back. I mean, when I play football, I can score a touchdown *every* time. Sometimes I'd love to just cut loose and do what I can do."

When he looked at me just then, his eyes sparkled. Josiah was changing. Before he'd been unhappy, but now he loved life. I was glad to see that change, and felt very good because I knew I was the one who'd made it happen.

Despite my happiness, I was troubled too. Josiah no longer needed to hide his true nature around me, but I still hid the real me from him. I yearned to tell him the truth, but I feared risking my only friendship with another boy.

"Out with it," said Josiah.

"Out with what?"

"It's back again, that look on your face. Every time we start to really have fun together, it shows up. Something is hurting you, Graham. Tell me what it is and maybe I can help."

I looked at him. I had no idea my thoughts showed so clearly on my face. I wanted to tell Josiah everything, but I was afraid. What if I confessed my darkest secrets and Josiah hated me for it? What if I lost him, just when everything was going so well?

I just stood there silent for a few moments, feeling the wind on my face, listening to the birds chirping in the near distance, smelling the newly mown grass at our feet. Everything was so perfect I didn't want to ruin it. I didn't want anything to change. Then again, I wanted things to change with Josiah, if they'd go my way. I wanted Josiah to be my boyfriend.

"I'm afraid you wouldn't understand."

"I've been around for a long time, Graham, there isn't much I can't understand."

"I'm just afraid…I'm afraid you won't like me, if I tell you about me."

"Graham, I like you. Nothing is going to change that. Come on. Let me help you."

"I'm gay!" I blurted it out before fear had a chance to silence me. I wanted to say more, but I my courage failed. I looked at Josiah in fear. I was actually more afraid at that moment than I was at any time in the past, and that was saying something.

"Awesome," said Josiah.

I just looked at him for a moment, my eyes wide and my mouth gaping. Had he really said what I thought he did? I heard the word plainly enough, but it was the last word I expected to hear.

"Awesome?" I asked.

"Yeah, awesome, as in great, fantastic, wonderful." Josiah was smiling at me.

"You don't mind?"

"Do I sound like I mind?"

"Well, no."

"Well, then, you have your answer."

I was shocked into silence. I'd pictured a hundred different possibilities and this wasn't one of them. I felt as if the weight of the world was lifted from my shoulders. Even knowing that Bry was out to get me didn't seem important anymore. I'd never felt so free. I very nearly told Josiah how I felt about him, but I didn't want to push it. I also came close to asking Josiah if he was gay too, but it just didn't seem the right time. No matter. I'd just revealed my deepest, most closely kept secret to Josiah and he still liked me! I smiled from ear to ear. I did something I'd never done before too, I hugged Josiah. He hugged me back. It was the most wonderful feeling in the entire world.

※ ※ ※

Josiah met me at the end of Mr. Diggory's lane every day after work. I knew he was there to watch over me, but he was also there just to *be* with me. Almost overnight, we'd become great friends. Josiah was at my house all the time. My days of being a lonely boy were over. My grades improved dramatically too, because Josiah was helping me study. I realized just how brilliant he was as he helped me through difficult subjects.

"You've read every book, haven't you?" I asked him one evening while he was helping me with a social studies assignment.

"Well, not *every* book, but a lot of them."

"How many, do you think?"

"Um, I don't know really. Thousands at least."

Having a friend who had been around for centuries was definitely a big help when it came to social studies. Josiah looked fifteen, but he'd been around for ages. I don't think I truly grasped that fact until I had to do an essay on the Battle of Gettysburg, explaining what I thought it was like for the soldiers who fought there.

"Good job," said Josiah after he'd read my essay, "It's well written and descriptive, but you need to mention how terrifying it was with the bullets whizzing through the air, all around, killing others so near you could hear the bullet going in. And the cannons, walking into the cannons as they fired, so many of them, all pouring forth smoke and flame and death. And the stench…sometimes it was unbearable."

I was gazing at him as he spoke.

"You were there? Weren't you?" I asked him.

"Yes. I was there. I was too young to fight, but I was a Union drummer boy…The Confederates were using boys as young as me, and younger, to fight in battles, but the Union didn't do that so much. I know boys my age were fighting on both sides, but I didn't really want to fight. I didn't want to kill anyone. Still, it was hard not to be a part of things, and so I became a drummer boy…"

I listened with rapt attention as Josiah told me what it was really like. I'd always thought battles were glorious and somehow romantic, but I quickly learned they were terrible and tragic. Josiah made it all so clear for me that I felt as if I were there. I completely rewrote my essay. I got an A+ on it too.

※ ※ ※

"Graham, your father and I need to speak with you," said Mom after I'd returned from Mr. Diggory's. Josiah was with me, as usual. Mom looked at him a bit suspiciously. It made both of us uncomfortable.

"Um…I'd better be going," said Josiah.

"Okay…Well, see you tomorrow."

"Yeah, bye, Graham."

Mom watched Josiah leave; her face grim.

I followed Mom into the living room. She took a seat on the couch next to Dad. I sat across from them, wondering what was up. I just sat there looking at them.

"We'd like you to explain this," said my dad, opening one of my notebooks to reveal an entire page covered with the name "Josiah", most of them inside little hearts. I gulped and my heart lurched in my chest.

"I…uh…" I didn't know what to say. I was so embarrassed I wanted to sink into the couch and disappear.

"Are you gay, Graham?" asked my dad.

A million thoughts ripped through my head in an instant. *I don't want my parents to know I'm gay. Dad's gonna kill me. Why didn't I keep my notebook hidden? Are they still going to love me if I tell them the truth? Can I just lie my way outta this? How am I going to explain the notebook? Maybe I can say it's Kelly's, but it's in my handwriting. I don't want to live a lie. I want to be proud of myself. What if they won't let me see Josiah anymore? Is Dad gonna hit me? Maybe I can just die right now and not have to deal with this. I wish I could just disappear or become invisible. I'm not going to be a coward—I'm gonna tell 'em.*

"Yes," I said finally. I couldn't believe I'd said it, but I said it. *Oh my God, I just told my parents I'm gay!*

Mom looked stricken, like maybe I'd just announced that I had cancer or something. Dad was angry.

"You're too young to know if you're gay or not," he stated flatly.

"Then why did you ask me?" I said.

"I will not have a gay son!"

"Well, you've got one, Dad—me!" I couldn't believe I had the balls to say that, or to raise my voice to my father. He slapped my face and tears stung my eyes.

"Alex!" yelled my mom, clearly shaken that Dad had slapped me.

"What have you been doing with that boy?" asked Dad, angrily.

"Nothing!" I said.

"Don't lie to me!"

"We don't do anything. We just hang out. We run and play basketball and stuff. He helps me study."

"Yeah, I'm sure he studies you. How old is he, Graham? Fifteen? Sixteen?"

"He's fifteen."

"He's brainwashed you, hasn't he? What's he been doing to you, Graham?"

"Nothing! He's not been doing anything to me!"

Dad put his hands on my shoulders, "I want you to tell me the truth, Graham. Have the two of you had sex?"

"Dad!"

"Answer me."

"No! We haven't done anything like that. Josiah doesn't even know I'm in love with him!"

"Do NOT say that!"

"Why not? It's true!" I simply couldn't believe I had the balls to stand up to my father like that. I never thought I'd be able to do that, not ever.

Dad slapped my face again, hard. It was an open hand slap, but it stung.

"It's not true! You are not a queer! I won't let you be a queer!"

"I'm gay!"

Dad slapped my face again.

"Alex! Stop it!" said my mom. Dad hitting me had snapped her out of her shock.

"Go pack a bag," said Dad. Tears welled up in my eyes. This was it. They were gonna kick me out.

"Why?"

"We're going to get you some help. There are places where they can undo whatever it is that boy's done to you."

"No!"

"Now, Graham!"

I just stood there, horrified. I'd heard of those places he was talking about. I didn't know much about them at all, but I imagined it was like being sent to Hell.

"Go!"

I turned on my heel and walked upstairs, trembling. I packed a backpack like Dad said, but I sure as hell wasn't going where he planned to take me. No way! Dad looked in on me and seemed satisfied that I was doing what I was told. I packed up a good supply of clothes, all the money I could find, a couple of books, deodorant, soap, a washcloth and towel, my tooth brush and tooth paste, everything I could think of that I might need. Mom came into the room while I was packing.

"Honey," she said, mussing my hair. I pulled away from her.

"Your father's just angry now. He's sorry he hit you. He won't do it again. He's just worried, Graham. We just want to help you through this."

"Then accept me for what I am," I said. "Love me."

"We do love you, Graham."

"So you're sending me away?" There was a lump in my throat. Despite what Mom was saying, I felt like my parents didn't love me.

"Just for a little while. Everything's going to be fine. You'll see. Your father has already found a nice place where they'll help you, down in Kentucky. It's called *The Cloverdale Center*. They help boys and girls like you all the time. You'll like it there."

How did she know what that place was like? She'd never even heard of it until a few minutes ago. I was sure it was a place I didn't want to be. I was NOT going. I had to save myself, so for the time being, I held my tongue and pretended to cooperate. Mom ruffled my hair and I let her.

"Come down for supper, Graham. It's too late to take you now, so we'll have supper, get a good nights sleep, then we'll check this place out in the morning. You'll see, Graham. Everything's going to be okay."

She talked like she really meant it. Maybe she did, but she sure didn't know what she was talking about. I wasn't going to let some shrink get his hands on me and screw with my head. I didn't know much about such places, but I'd heard they were bad. Billy Durex had been sent there last year, rumor was because he was gay. No one had seen Billy since and his family hadn't moved. No way was I going in there.

I nodded at my mom and followed her downstairs. I sat down to supper with my parents, but I felt like I was eating with strangers. I stuffed myself. I ate until I was ready to explode. I knew I might not get regular meals for who knew how long.

After supper, I sat in my room and did homework as if all was well. I made sure I had everything packed that I might possibly need, right down to some loose change I kept in the bottom of one of my dresser drawers.

My mom tucked me in for the night and turned out my light. I lay there until I was sure that she and Dad were asleep, then I crept out of the bed, grabbed my backpack, and climbed out the window. I noiselessly slipped to the ground, put my pack on my shoulders, and double-checked to make sure I had the little bag of lemon balm around my neck. I'd already decided where I'd hide. I set out for the *Forest Grove Amusement Park.*

I hurried along. I felt vulnerable out in the open. Bry was out there somewhere and so were the twins and who knew how many others. Even if they weren't looking for me, I didn't want to risk a chance meeting. I was no match for a vampire. I thought that maybe I should go to Josiah, instead of hiding out in the amusement park. I didn't feel right about it, though. Maybe I would go to him after I got everything sorted out, but for now I just needed to get away from home and decide on my next move.

The sudden uncertainty of my life frightened me. Never before had I been homeless. I'd always gotten up in the morning, had breakfast, then gone to school. In the afternoon, I'd come home, do whatever, then go to bed and get up the next day. I worked for Basil and sometimes I went out for fun, but everything in my life had been stable. I knew where I'd be the next day, the next week, the next year. Now all that was gone. I couldn't go back home. My parents wanted to send me to that awful place. I didn't really have anywhere else to go, though. I was thirteen and definitely wasn't ready to make my own way in the world. I made good money working for Mr. Diggory, but how far would that go when I had to pay for food and clothes and all that?

My lower lip trembled as I realized I couldn't work for Basil anymore. My parents knew I worked for him and they'd go there looking for me. I couldn't even go to school again. Mom and Dad would surely show up there when they discovered I was missing. I felt lost and alone. I was shaking with fear and it wasn't just because there were vampires about. *Let's just get to Forest Grove, Graham, and settle in, then we'll work it all out*, I thought to myself.

I didn't get my flashlight out until I was walking around the outside of the fence, trying to find the opening near the back once again. I slipped through the opening and entered *Forest Grove*, my new home. The clouds rolled in and deepened the darkness. It began to sprinkle rain as I passed the drink stand and the bench where I'd sat not so many days ago. I passed the funnel cake stand and the Tilt-A-Whirl. Not so distant lightning rent the sky, shattering the darkness with brilliant light. I followed the path uphill, passing the little Indian canoe ride for kids and the big open-air Mexican restaurant. It all looked so eerie, deserted, and dark. I remembered *Forest Grove* as a place of sunshine and laughter. Now it was all darkness and desolation. On my left were the bumper cars, as still and silent as the rest of the park. I followed the path to my right, walking between the carnival games on my right and the space where the spider ride had been to my left. Straight on was the old gift shop. I quickened my pace as the rain came down harder and the wind began to blow. The doors to the gift shop were locked, of course, but I managed to pry open a window.

It was dark inside, no surprise there, but what did astound me was the fact that the gift shop was still stocked just as it had been when I'd been there so long ago. The beam of my flashlight revealed racks of dusty *Forest Grove* t-shirts, souvenir cups, plates, and trays. There was a rotating rack of postcards on the counter, next to jars of moldy candy and *Forest Grove* buttons and pencils. The place looked untouched; I wondered why it hadn't been looted. It sure wasn't too hard for me to break in.

The counter formed a large square near the center of the shop. I pushed open the swinging half-door and put my backpack down inside. There was carpet on the floor and I felt secure in that small space. The wind and rain raged outside, but I was warm and dry. It was almost comfy in there.

The gift shop was a good place to hide. No one would suspect I'd be hiding out in *Forest Grove*. If Bry was looking for me, he'd be hanging around my house or the route I traveled to school. He wouldn't think to look on the opposite side of town in an abandoned amusement park. My parents weren't likely to look for me there either, but I wasn't taking any chances. I intended to stay well out of sight.

I made myself a little bed on the floor with the sleeping bag I'd carried along. Tomorrow was a school day, but I wouldn't be going, so I could sleep in as long as I wanted. Oddly enough, I already missed school. I missed my old life. I'd always thought my life sucked, but now that it was gone, it didn't seem so bad after all.

I clutched the bag of lemon balm hanging around my neck tightly and fell asleep listening to the wind whipping the rain around outside.

🍁   🍁   🍁

I awakened with the morning light peeking through the dirty windows of the gift shop. A quick glance at my watch told me it was a little after nine. My parents knew I was gone by now and were no doubt looking for me. I was a wanted man now. I figured I was reasonably safe from detection as long as I didn't leave the park, but I was still uneasy.

I stretched and pulled a chewy granola bar out of my backpack for breakfast. After gobbling it down, I went outside and sat on a bench looking in the direction of the bumper cars and the bumper boat pool across from them. I sat there and had a good long think about my future. I was definitely in a fix. I couldn't stick around too long or I'd be found, but I didn't want to run away either. I'd seen news stories about what happened to runaways. I'd end up in some big city somewhere, probably selling myself for something to eat. I didn't want that kind of life. Besides, I knew I wasn't tough enough to make it in the big, bad world. The main reason I didn't want to leave was Josiah. He was the only guy friend I'd ever had and I didn't want to lose him. More than that, I was in love with him; the idea of parting was just unthinkable.

But how could I stay? If I did, my parents would cart me away to that center and they'd mess with my mind. Who knew what I'd be like when I came back, and would I even come back? Even if that place was on the up and up, I didn't want to change. I wanted to be me. Being gay was a part of what I was and to change that would be to destroy the boy that I was. I was sure it wasn't on the up and up, however. If I went in there they'd probably torture me or something. I didn't like pain.

I wished Josiah was with me. He'd know what to do. I probably should've gone straight to him instead of coming to the park, but I needed to sort things out. The more I thought about it, the more it seemed like Josiah was my only salvation. With his help, I could get away and I'd be with him too. Maybe it'd be like it was with Josiah and Zac. We could travel the world together and see and do all kinds of incredible things. Best of all, I'd be with him always. I loved him and I already missed him.

I wanted to go and see Josiah that very moment, but he'd be in school. I wondered what he'd think when I didn't show up for lunch. Would he just suspect I was sick or something, or would he come looking for me? I couldn't risk going to school to see him. They'd be looking for me there. I didn't dare go into town at all. The cops were no doubt searching for me and, at the very least, my parents would be looking around. I quickly made up my mind to go to Josiah, but it would have to wait until dark. I couldn't risk anyone spotting me. All I could do was wait until night. I didn't like the idea of going out at night, the most dangerous time I could pick with vampires on the prowl, but I had no choice but to seek the cover of darkness. At nightfall I'd be on my way, but until then I dared not leave the park.

CHAPTER 13

※

Lurking in the Lair

I had hours to kill before I could attempt to make it to Josiah. There was nothing to do but explore the park, so I got up from the bench where I was sitting and walked up the paved path. It took a little turn to the right and a long, low building came into view. Actually, it was more than one building hooked together. It had almost a European look to it and over one section was a sign that read *Black Forest Café*. I tried the door and it was open. Inside was a long counter. I remembered it being a lot taller as I'd stood there with my parents, ordering pizza, I think, on our last visit. There were tables and chairs all about, many of them overturned. I grew sad thinking about all the people who'd eaten there once. It seemed such a shame for the place to go to waste. I don't think I'd have been nearly as sad if I didn't remember being there myself so very well. I'd been there in the summer and the whole place was filled with bright light and people eating and laughing; taking a break from riding on the roller coasters, the train, the log ride, the bumper cars, and all the other rides in the park. Now I was standing there alone on a gloomy day; all those laughing faces were gone. The feeling returned to me that I'd had when I'd visited the park several days before; the feeling of being alone in the world.

I went outside, but it was only slightly less gloomy there. In the near distance I could see the ticket booths and on my right was the skeet-ball building I'd noticed from outside the fence. The asphalt path took a turn down and to the right. Only a few feet along, a path branched to the left. This was the part of the park I remembered the best. It was the kiddy section where I'd had such fun when I was six or seven. There was a little merry-go-round there, as well as a miniature version of the bumper boats. The merry-go-round was gone now and all that remained of the little bumper boats was the empty pool. I smiled when I walked over to the airplane ride. It was just sitting there as if it were awaiting the next kid to climb on. Eight little airplanes were attached by chains to the roof. I loved that ride when I was a kid. When it started up, the planes flew round and round, raising higher with each turn. I remembered feeling like I was really flying on that ride! I was too big to fit in the planes now, even if the park had still been open.

I felt a joyous sadness in my heart. It's a feeling that's hard to describe. I was both happy and sad at the same time. Walking around the amusement park where I'd had such fun as a kid brought back pleasant memories, but I was saddened by the fact that the park was closed. No more would those little airplanes fly around. No more would the merry-go-round play its cheerful music.

I looked up to see *The Jaguar* towering over me. A section of the giant roller coaster went right by the Kiddy area. I'd never ridden *The Jaguar*, nor *The Wolf*, an even bigger roller coaster not far away in the park. I was too short for either of them; I didn't measure up to the *You Must Be This Tall To Ride* sign. I was tall enough now, but it was too late. No matter, I'd have been too scared to ride them anyway.

I left the kiddy area and followed the winding path down the hill. The asphalt branched off and I followed the path to the left. It led down to *The Fearful Falls*, the old log ride. I grinned remembering it. It was my favorite ride in the whole park. I'd been too small to ride it by myself, but I was just tall enough that I could go on it with my dad. I remembered it like it was yesterday. It was such a blast! There was a dark tunnel at the beginning of the ride, then it rushed along a narrow stream, past an old "graveyard", then on up a big rollercoaster-like incline before hurtling down to create a tremendous splash in the small river of water at the bottom. I looked down at the now dry "stream" and the empty logs. I wished more than anything that the old park wasn't closed. It seemed such a shame for it all to sit there unused.

I headed back up to where the path had split and walked right up to *The Wolf*. The massive roller coaster dominated that entire area of the park. It was the largest wooden roller coaster in the whole country in its time, but now it sat silent. It seemed impossibly tall; a mountain of crisscrossing wooden beams. How they ever managed to construct the thing, I couldn't even imagine. Just looking at the first huge incline made me dizzy. It went up and up like it'd never stop.

I don't think I'd have ridden *The Wolf* even if the park was still open. I was rather terrified of heights. I did remember the way it sounded, however. It was odd; I didn't want to ride it, but I loved listening to it. Like everything else in the park, it was now silent.

It amazed me that so many of the rides were still just sitting there. Some of them, like *The Fearful Falls, The Jaguar,* and *The Wolf* obviously couldn't be moved at all, but others, like the Tilt-A-Whirl and *The Artic Circle* wouldn't have been that hard to put on a truck and move to another park somewhere. So far, the only rides there were entirely missing were that spider ride, and the Merry-Go-Round from the kiddy area. The whole place was a big mess, but with a little work it could have become an operating amusement park again. The place definitely needed cleaned up. The paths were littered with a few seasons worth of fall leaves and every window was clouded and dusty. I wished it could all be as it once was.

Across from *The Wolf* was a big arcade with carnival games on the outside facing the coaster. The arcade part was locked up tight, but the game stalls were standing open. The stillness of the place gave it an oppressive air. I sat down on a bench and bowed my head. Something about being in a place where I'd once been so happy made the pain of recent events that much more intense. I couldn't believe how my parents had reacted when I'd told them I was gay. I felt like they didn't love me anymore. I wouldn't let myself think about it. I got up and explored some more, filling the empty hours until I could seek Josiah's help.

I wandered down to the *Raging Rapids* raft ride. It was my favorite, next to *The Fearful Falls*; maybe I even liked it a little bit more. I couldn't decide. I stepped under the tin roof that covered the waiting area. The zigzagging line had enough room for a couple of hundred people or so. It was eerie being there all alone. The water channel was dry, of course, so I stepped down into it and walked where once I'd ridden a huge, round, eight-person raft.

At the very beginning, there was a long, curving tunnel, painted black. For several feet I couldn't see anything at all and had to feel my way forward, then a dim gray light appeared as I rounded the corner, slowly brightening into the full light of day. It was still cloudy and dreary, but it seemed almost bright outside compared to the tunnel. I wandered on down the channel, thinking how much more fun it'd been in a raft, with water splashing all over. At last I came to the little western town at the bottom of the hill. It had the appearance of a flooded town when there was water in the channel, but it was dry as could be now.

The town was cool, even if it was only storefronts. There was a saloon, a livery stable, a boot shop, and even an undertaker. At the end of the town the channel passed right through the old saloon. It was the only building that had any kind of interior. There was an old chandelier overhead, a bar along one wall, and even a piano. It seemed real, even though I knew it was created just for fun. I followed the channel back to the beginning and continued to explore the park. The minutes were crawling by; I didn't think night would ever come.

I went back to the gift shop where I'd left my backpack and pulled out a couple more chewy granola bars for lunch. Luckily, the water fountains in the park still worked and were clean, cool, and clear. After I'd eaten, I lay down and had myself a little nap.

🍁   🍁   🍁

The evening shadows had come at last. I'd wandered around the old amusement park all day. There was lots to explore, but the emptiness and silence made me feel lonely and gloomy. I wondered where my parents were and if they missed me. Was my dad sorry he'd slapped me, or was he just glad I was gone? I felt like there was only one person I could trust and that was Josiah. If only darkness would come so I could seek him out.

I sat on a bench by *The Wolf* as the shadows deepened. The silence was even more pronounced as the sun sank into the west. When the sound of voices came to my ears, it had a dream-like quality and at first I wasn't sure if the voices were real or imagined. My eyes grew wide and my heart pounded in my chest as the voices became clearer. I jumped from the bench and hurtled myself over the counter of the ring-toss game. I hid myself under the counter while fighting to control my rapid breathing and the terror that had seized me. The voices; I recognized them. It was the twins! What were they doing here?

The voices grew nearer and nearer, then stopped. I was panic-stricken. My heart jolted when there was a large thud on the counter above me. I fearfully looked up; there was Clay smiling evilly at me, staring down at me with his bright eyes. He hopped to the floor and jerked me to my feet before I could so much as scream. He hauled me from behind the counter, his fingers digging painfully into my arm. He pushed me toward Jay, who wrapped his arms around me in a vice-like grip. I struggled, but it was useless. The twins had always been stronger than me, but now I couldn't budge Jay's arms at all.

"Look what we have here, Jay," said Clay. "It looks like a little Graham wandering around in *our* amusement park."

I struggled, but it was of absolutely no use whatsoever. I looked into Clay's eyes. He was delighted.

"How nice of you to come visit us, Graham. How did you know this was our meeting place? Your buddy, Bry, will be here soon. He's eager to see you, Graham, most eager."

I swallowed hard. This was the end. I'd gambled and I'd lost. I had no chance at all to break away and escape. I was doomed.

"We're going to have some real fun this time, Graham. No simple bullying or beating for you. This time is for keeps."

"You know," whispered Jay right into my ear "I could just crush your chest." He started tightening his arms more and more. It was if an anaconda had wrapped itself around me. The air was forced from my lungs and my ribs pressed inward. I fought to inhale, but I couldn't pull in any air. Every time I exhaled in an attempt to breathe, Jay's hold tightened. I felt myself turning purple as I began to making a sound somewhere between gagging and choking. I couldn't breathe at all. The pressure on my chest was so intense I expected the bones to start snapping at any moment. Jay kept tightening until I was on the verge of passing out. He loosened his grip and I gasped for air.

"Yes, this is going to be a lot of fun," said Clay, grinning. I swallowed hard. "But business before pleasure." Clay's features became angry and frightening. He took my chin in his hand and forced me to look at him.

"How very fortunate for us to find you wandering around alone, and how very stupid of you. We've been watching for our chance, but that freak, Josiah, never leaves your side, does he?"

Clay punched me in the stomach so hard I thought my intestines had ruptured. I grunted loudly. I knew then that the twins weren't merely going to torment me. They were going to kill me.

Clay grabbed my hair and pulled my head to one side, baring my neck. I was hyperventilating with pure terror. I'd have begged him to spare me, but I couldn't speak. I squirmed to free myself, but it was useless; Jay's grip was unbreakable.

Clay bared his fangs and hissed into my face. A moment later, he sank his long, sharp fangs into the base of my neck, near the shoulder. I cried out in pain. He drew back not long after and smiled at me. My blood dripping from his lips.

"You'll soon be one of us, Graham. Nothing can save you now." He laughed in my face.

"And now," said Clay, "to complete our task."

Jay released me with his tight grasp, twisted me around, and gripped my pectoral muscles with his hands, just under my armpits. He began to squeeze and I cried out in pain.

"You're going to have to scream louder than that for him to hear you," said Jay.

I jerked my head up and looked into his eyes.

"That's right, Graham, you're the bait. What's more, you're going to help us get rid of Josiah. He's too powerful for us to manage it alone, but you are his weakness, Graham. He'll let down his guard to save you."

"No," I said, turning my head from side to side. "I'll never help you!"

"Oh, but you will, Graham. You already have, by letting yourself be captured so easily. Now we can do what needed to be done all along. Josiah is dangerous and must be destroyed."

"He's only dangerous to you!" I cried, still in pain. "You're the ones who should be destroyed! Just wait. Josiah will kick your ass. He'll destroy you both."

"Will he? Call him then. Call him and we'll see."

I wanted more than anything to call for help, but I feared the results. If Clay was so intent on my calling Josiah, then it couldn't be good. I remained silent.

"I'm growing impatient," hissed Clay. "Call him, scream for him to come, Graham."

Jay squeezed my pectoral muscles with unbearable force. I had to fight with all my might not to scream out loud. Tears rolled down my cheeks and I groaned in pain.

"Scream for me, Graham. Scream for me or it only gets worse." Clay grabbed me too, and I felt pain like I'd never felt before. I was using every ounce of strength I had not to cry out, but I couldn't do it. It was too excruciating. I screamed in agony, louder than I'd ever screamed before.

I fell limp into Clay's arms, tears streaming from my eyes; tears of pain and remorse. I should have held my tongue. I should have kept silent, no matter what, but I just wasn't strong enough.

"Good boy, Graham. You've played your part well. Now all we have to do is wait for Josiah. I always thought you were useless, Graham, but you're the perfect hostage, so weak and vulnerable, so easy to control. When Josiah gets here…"

A loud whoosh of wings came from above and Angelica landed on a branch not far above me. At the same moment, something rammed into Clay even as he gloated. His hold on me was broken. The force of the attack knocked me to the ground. I looked up to see a black wolf with bright blue eyes on top of Clay biting him viciously. As I watched it transformed into Josiah and kept fighting. Clay was fighting back, but he was no match for Josiah. I knew it would be over in mere moments.

Jay looked horrified. I knew that whatever plan he and Clay had concocted had gone horribly wrong. Josiah had arrived much too quickly. Jay wasn't finished just yet, however. Before I could even think of escaping, he grabbed me and lifted me off the ground with his powerful arms. I struggled, but it was useless. Jay put one hand on each side of my head and shouted, "Stop or I'll kill him, Josiah!"

Josiah froze. He stood and turned, leaving Clay laying on the ground, moaning. He took one step forward.

"Oh, that's not a good idea at all, Josiah. Take one more step and I'll crush his skull like a walnut."

Jay increased the pressure and I felt as if my skull could crack at any moment. I tried not to cry out, but I was in such pain I couldn't help it. It made me feel weak and pathetic. I hated myself for it, and I hated Jay. Even though I could not see him standing behind me, I knew he was smiling. I'd have given anything to wipe that smile off his face.

"Now, we'll just stand here and wait," said Jay.

I knew what he was waiting for, or rather who—Bry. Perhaps others were coming too, but Bry was a far more powerful vampire than either of the twins. With his help...I didn't even want to think about it.

I heard a horrible growl and a great, hairy wolf slammed Josiah to the ground. Josiah fended it off. As I watched, the wolf became Bry and he and Josiah rolled around in the leaves. Clay pulled himself up and pounced on Josiah too. He was outnumbered and it was all my fault.

I fought to free myself from Jay's grasp, but he was so many times stronger than me that I didn't stand a chance against him. I had to do something. I couldn't just stand there and watch. I scrambled to think of something, anything, I could do to get away. In a few moments, I thought of something. I did the one thing I could think of doing. I raised my knee and jammed my heel into Jay's foot with as much force as I could muster. He cried out in pain and released me.

I rolled away as soon as I hit the ground. I pulled out the lemon balm I carried with me always and shoved it at Clay as he grabbed for me again. I knew I couldn't let him get me. If he did, he could use me to control Josiah. Clay lunged and hissed at me, but he couldn't get close enough to lay his hands on me. I fended him off with a simple herb that grew in Basil's garden. Jay screamed in anger. He turned from me and attacked Josiah.

I saw Clay go flying through the air. Josiah threw him farther than I'd ever seen anyone thrown. The impact should have killed Clay, but he got up and launched himself at Josiah once again. Clay and Jay rammed into Josiah at the same time and smashed him back against a tree trunk. It should have crushed him, but the only visible effect was that it made him angrier than before.

The fight that followed was terrible to see. The twins and Bry viciously attacked Josiah, intent on destroying him. He was outnumbered three to one and I could not help. The twins had so abused my body that every movement was painful. Even if I was undamaged, I did not possess the strength of a vampire.

My neck throbbed and I reached up to feel it. I felt sick. I was growing weaker by the second. Soon I'd be of no use to Josiah, whatsoever. I took a deep breath, grasped the lemon balm firmly in hand and pounced on Clay's back. I didn't try to strike him, I just shoved the herb right into his face. I held it on him. He screamed and flung me to the ground like a puppet. The lemon balm went flying. He lunged for me, but Josiah rammed him with his shoulder and sent him flying backward into a tree. His arm twisted behind him and he screamed.

I scrambled to my feet and bolted with explosive speed. I knew the best thing I could do to help Josiah was to get away. I was no match for vampires and all I could do was be a liability. Even in his damaged state, Clay just missed grabbing me and was nearly on my heels. I tried to break to the right, but Josiah and Bry were rolling on the ground, with Jay lunging at Josiah. I was forced to take the only route open to me; the waiting line for *The Wolf.*

I scrambled under and over the chains that formed the line, fearing every second that Clay would catch up to me. He was so close behind I could hear his labored breathing. The fight with Josiah had taken a great deal out of him and so had the lemon balm. I dashed up the wooden stairs and onto the covered track. Clay jumped onto them only moments later.

My heart pounded in fear as I began to run—up the first great incline of the coaster. There was a narrow walkway on one side, probably used by maintenance crews, and up it I ran. The climb was so steep that soon I was nearly bent double, using my hands to steady myself as I climbed forty, fifty, then sixty feet in the air. I was trembling with terror and only part of it came from Clay pursuing me. I was absolutely terrified of heights and yet I was climbing higher and higher with each step.

My breath was coming so fast and hard that I was dizzy. I tried to calm myself and slow my breathing rate down. The last thing I needed was to pass out dozens of feet from the ground. I felt weak and shaky as my legs took me up and up. I was more than a hundred feet off the ground now, and still climbing. Clay wasn't far behind.

Far below me I could see Bry and Jay as they pounced upon Josiah once more. He was in trouble; Bry's strength was nearly a match for his own and he had Jay to contend with besides. At least I was keeping Clay busy, but I didn't know how long I could fend him off. I felt myself growing weaker and my heart felt like it would explode in my chest. My body was failing and my mind was on the verge of launching into a panic attack. I was becoming hysterical with fear. I was nearly at the highest point of the incline and I felt as if I were already falling. I looked at the ground far, far below. I felt like I was a mile in the sky. I cried out in terror, but kept climbing higher. If I stopped, even for a moment, Clay would have me.

I watched the fight below as I climbed. Bry launched himself at Josiah, but Josiah threw him off with such force that Bry went crashing into the very carnival game booth where I'd been hiding. It gave way under his weight. Bry cried out in pain. He didn't come back at Josiah. He'd had enough.

Jay jumped upon Josiah's back, as Bry fled into the darkness. Jay was no match for Josiah alone, however. Josiah threw him off and Jay backed away from him, knowing he could not match him in strength.

I groaned in pain and collapsed across the track of the coaster. My strength had all but left me. My vision swirled in and out and I knew I was dying. I cursed myself for being weak. I'd brought Josiah into the trap with my pitiful cries. I should have held them in and died silent. It had hurt so very much though, worse than anything I'd ever experienced. I just couldn't help it. Still, I felt a failure as my life ebbed away.

I heard a horrible anguished scream and jerked my head to the side to see Jay pinned to the ground with a large splintered piece of wood. Blood was everywhere. My vision blacked out for a moment and when it came back Jay's head was separated from his body. His torso began to smoke and wither; looking as though he were boiling, turning inside out. The sight was so horrible, so gruesome, that I had to look away. When I looked back once more, there was nothing left but his steaming clothing.

Clay was upon me. I lay on my back looking up at him. His face was blistered on one side where I'd touched him with the lemon balm. His right arm hung at an odd angle, broken in his fight with Josiah. He looked down upon me in murderous rage.

"You don't deserve to be one of us!" he hissed as he grabbed the front of my shirt and lifted me clear of the track.

My legs dangled beneath me as Clay carried me to the railing. We were at the top now, with a drop of more than two hundred feet below us. My heart clutched in terror and my body began to spasm; whether from some change that was taking place within me or from some fear induced seizure, I didn't know.

Clay lifted me higher, intent on tossing me to my death. It seemed a waste of time really: I could feel myself already dying. My vision swirled, blackened, then snapped out as if I'd gone blind. In a moment more I felt consciousness slipping from me. My last thought was that at least I'd be unaware of the horrible fall.

I awakened sometime later. I could have been out for days, but it seemed only moments had passed. Clay was nowhere to be seen and Josiah hovered over me.

"Come!" he said. "There isn't much time. It may be too late already. Come!"

He pulled me to my feet. I was so weak I was like a rag doll; limp, my head lulling from side to side. Josiah lifted me onto his shoulders without effort and ran with the speed of the wind, and faster than that. We were off the coaster in a blink of the eye and then the forest went by in a total blur. I knew I was traveling far faster than I ever had before, in mere moments we were at our destination. I was amazed when I saw where Josiah had taken me.

CHAPTER 14

❈

Death's Doorstep

Basil opened the door quickly and Josiah carried me inside. One look at me was all Basil needed to know I was in serious trouble.

"Put him on my bed," said Basil. "What happened?"

"He's been bitten—again," said Josiah. "Can you stop it? Are we in time?"

Basil pushed my hair back and felt my forehead. He peered deeply into my eyes. I could barely see him; it was if I were peering at him through a misty fog. He probed the wounds on my neck. I felt light headed and weak, and my stomach and legs ached. Basil's countenance was grave.

"I will be back in a few moments, don't let him go to sleep."

I knew that I was not going to be harmed. I trusted Josiah completely. I trusted Basil completely too. The look on Josiah's face terrified me, however. He was so upset he was about to cry. I knew that I must be very bad off for him to look like that. I knew I must be close to death. I felt as if I was too.

"What's wrong?" I asked. "What's happening to me? I feel so weak and I'm beginning to hurt all over." I grimaced in pain and my body convulsed.

"You've been bitten three times by a vampire. You are changing. You're becoming one of them."

My eyes widened. I was becoming a vampire? Yes, one bite had no effect, neither did two, but three bites from a vampire brought with it transformation. I was doomed to become one of them.

"No!" I said. I meant to scream it, but my voice came out all weak and shaky.

"If anyone can stop it, Basil can. He's been working on this for decades," said Josiah, but he did not sound confident.

"Decades?" I asked.

I could not hear Josiah's response. I was fading. I was so very tired. All I wanted to do was sleep. I closed my eyes. Sleep—that's all I wanted just then. I was tired…so tired.

I felt Josiah slapping my face.

"Stay with me, Graham. Stay with me."

Basil entered the room carrying a steaming cup.

"More tea?" I feebly asked.

"Of a sort," said Basil.

Josiah positioned me so that my back was resting against the headboard. He held me in place. I no longer had the strength to move at all. My head lolled to the side and Josiah had to hold it up for me.

"I want you to drink this," said Basil. "It will burn and bring you great pain, but it is your only hope."

I didn't like the sound of that at all. It was like when the doctor told me something would sting a little and it hurt like hell. I wondered what this would do to me, since Basil had actually said it would be painful. I was frightened. I believed Basil when he said it was my only hope, however. I trusted him, and I could feel something horrible happening to my body.

Basil held the cup to my lips and he and Josiah poured the contents down my throat. It burned fiercely going down, not from the heat of the brew, but from something else. It had a bitter taste and smell and I could catch a waft of a lemony scent.

The moment the cup was drained I was seized by intense pain, as if my entire body was withering in flames. It also felt like someone had kicked me in the nuts as hard as he could and that pain had been duplicated in every part of me. I screamed and flailed on the bed with what little strength remained in me. Josiah held me down with ease. I was so weak I could hardly move, but I was writhing in agony nonetheless. I thought I was dying and all I could think was that I wanted to die as fast as I possibly could. Every second of pain was an eternity of torment. I don't think it would have hurt more if I was being skinned alive.

Slowly the pain lessened. I was in such horrible torment that any lessening of the pain was a source of sweet pleasure. Gradually it left me, gradually it became bearable, until finally it was nothing more than a dull ache.

I became aware that Basil was peering into my eyes again, and examining my wounds. I was only half aware of him. I felt as if I were in a dream. Images faded in and out, as did the sounds of Basil and Josiah talking. I could make only some of it out.

"Did it work?" asked Josiah. "Were we in time?"

"Only just," said Basil. "A few more seconds and it would have been too late."

The voices faded out and suddenly I could not breathe at all. My entire body trembled and convulsed. I bit my own tongue. I fought to breathe but it was as if there were no air. My eyes were open, but I could see only darkness. I could hear nothing. Had I gone deaf and blind? Was this the price of the cure? Those thoughts were with me only a moment more as I fought to draw breath. I felt hands on me and thought maybe I heard words, but they were so strange and broken up that I must have been imagining them. A bright light flared in my mind. I made one last attempt to breathe air that was not there, then sank into darkness.

I opened my eyes and saw that I was in Basil's little house. That was a good thing because it meant I was still alive. I could remember nothing about the time I was unconscious. My last memory was of trying desperately to breathe when there was no air.

My lips, mouth, and throat were very dry. My chest hurt, hell, my whole body ached. I felt very, very weak, but I could move my arms and legs just a little. I suddenly realized that I was able to see. I couldn't before I'd passed out. I wasn't blind. That was another good thing.

"How are you feeling, my boy?" asked Basil. I hadn't noticed him, even though he was sitting on the edge of the bed. I noted that I could hear him. I wasn't deaf. That was a good thing, too.

I tried to speak, but at first nothing came out. When I was able to speak my voice was very scratchy.

"I'm feeling thirsty," I said.

Basil smiled and produced a glass of cold water. He sat me up in bed and steadied the glass as I drank. I was still too weak to handle it by myself. The water tasted better than anything ever had.

"What happened?" I asked. My memory was all foggy and uncertain.

"We nearly lost you. The cure I gave you is one that is only used as a last resort. It's extremely powerful and very touchy stuff. I've been working to prefect it, but it's no easy task I assure you. The potion reversed the vampirism. We caught it in time to bring you back. Your body couldn't handle it, however. You went into convulsions and your body started shutting down. It was touch and go there for a bit and I must admit I didn't know for a while if you'd pull through, but you are made of pretty tough stuff it seems."

"So I'm not going to be a vampire?" I asked, wincing.

"No, we caught it in time. Any longer and it would have been too late. There would have been nothing I, nor anyone else could have done. We need not discuss that, however. That danger has passed."

I looked around the room.

"Where's Josiah?"

He is making you some tea, apricot I believe."

My head was swimming with questions, and just plain swimming. I could think of a thousand things I wanted to ask Basil, and Josiah.

Josiah came in at just that moment and handed me a cup of tea. He took Basil's place by my side and helped me to take a few sips. It was good. I realized that I was starving, but I didn't feel like my stomach could handle anything just then. I took another sip of tea.

"I have some things to attend to," said Basil. "I'll leave you in Josiah's capable hands." He smiled and left.

"How do you feel?" asked Josiah.

"I'm not dead. Other than that, I don't feel so hot."

"I can understand that."

"Thanks for saving me, Josiah."

"You're welcome, but I'm not sure I did such a good job of that. I should have been quicker."

"Josiah, this wasn't your fault. Without you, I'd be one of them. You saved my life." I reached out with very unsteady hands, took his hand, and kissed it. I couldn't think of any better way to show him how thankful I was. He smiled slightly.

"I'm so sorry," I said.

"For what?"

"For being stupid. For getting myself caught. I wasn't thinking. I should have come straight to you when I ran away." I could see a question in Josiah's eyes when I said, "ran away", but he didn't ask me about it just then.

"You should, indeed, have come to me, but it's okay, Graham."

"No, it's not. I almost got you killed."

"No. Bry and the others wanted to destroy me, but it would take more than three of them to do the job. I've been a vampire much longer than they. I'm much more powerful."

I was still at fault, but I was too tired to say more. Even though I'd just awakened, I was exhausted. The small movements I'd made had tired me out completely. Josiah helped me get comfortable and then I drifted off to sleep once more.

CHAPTER 15

❦

Josiah and his Son

I slept most of the next few days. I awakened now and then to find either Josiah or Basil watching over me. I had weird, feverish dreams as I slept, all about wolves and vampires and things I couldn't even remember. I couldn't quite focus on anything, even when I was awake.

One afternoon I awakened and felt more lucid that usual. Josiah was sitting near my bed, looking at me very concerned. He smiled when I opened my eyes.

"Decided to grace me with your presence, huh?" he asked.

"Yeah." I smiled slightly, but the truth was, I didn't feel well enough to smile. I lay there silent for a moment, then asked Josiah something that had been on my mind.

"How do you know Basil? And, how does he know so much about vampires?" When I could think, I'd been thinking a lot about those two things. I had no idea that Josiah knew Basil at all. Neither mentioned the other—not once. Basil also had a great many books on vampires, and apparently a great deal of knowledge about them. There was too much going on for mere coincidence.

"That is a very long story," said Josiah.

"I think I have time to hear it. I'm not exactly doin' anything right now," I said.

"Perhaps, I can give you the short version. Basil..." said Josiah slowly "is my son."

Although the movement caused me pain, I turned my head and looked at him.

"Your son?" I asked incredulously. "But how? He can't..." I realized as I spoke that I was still thinking of Josiah as if he were fifteen. I closed my mouth and let him explain.

"I met Basil's mother...Let me see...Basil is now eighty-seven...so about eighty-eight years ago. Her name was Rose, Rose Diggory. I never intended to let her get close to me, but she did. I was so lonely then, and she was kind to me. I'm not sure why she liked me at all. She was eighteen and, to her, I was a mere boy.

As Josiah spoke, I became upset. He'd met a girl. He'd had a son. I'd hoped, especially after he told me about Zachary, that he might someday be my boyfriend. I'd fallen in love with Josiah. Somewhere along the way, it had happened. I didn't know when, or how, but somewhere on our journey together my feelings for him had changed from friendship to love. His words were breaking my heart.

"I should not have let it happen, but one night, I was feeling so alone... Rose comforted me and held me. She kissed me and I responded to her, even though I had no real attraction to girls. We...slept together, and nine months later Basil was born."

I almost ignored Josiah's last words. Had he really said what I thought he did? Had he really said that he had no real attraction to girls?

Josiah's voice faltered. My attention was jerked back to him. I peered at him. His eyes were all watery. I knew something had gone wrong.

"Rose didn't make it. There were complications, and she died in childbirth." Josiah cried openly. I looked at him with pity.

"I never meant for Rose to get close to me, but she had become a friend. She was the first friend I'd had in a long time, the first since Zachary. What happened between us wasn't supposed to happen, but it did, and the price for it was her life."

"You were just friends then? You weren't married or anything?"

"No, we weren't married. I didn't care for Rose like that. I loved her, but as a friend only. What happened between us on the night that I fathered Basil was an accident. Rose sought to comfort me and it got out of hand. She made me feel so loved."

"I'm so sorry she died," I said.

"Basil was such a beautiful baby," said Josiah. "I was heartbroken over the death of Rose, but she had given me something I never thought I'd have—a son. He was the joy of my life. I took him away with me and raised him alone.

"Basil started asking questions when he was old enough. He wanted to know why I looked so very young. I sat him down one day and told him the truth. At first, the thought I was teasing him, but I was able to prove it. He was shocked, but it changed nothing between us and for that I was glad.

"Basil's adolescence were turbulent years, not aided by the fact that I appeared to be the same age as he. It was during those years, however, that he took a great interest in chemistry and herbology. I didn't know it for a long time, but his interest was created by a desire to help me. Even though he was young, Basil understood the pain of being a vampire, and immortal. I did not speak of it, but he was observant, and inquisitive. He was so voracious in his collecting of vampire material that I feared someone would grow suspicious, but all seemed to take it as merely the interest of a boy fascinated by monsters.

"Basil left for college and I was once again alone. I began to wander about the world once more, but we always kept in touch and I visited him often. His friends at college knew me as his little brother.

"Eventually, Basil settled down here. I came to visit him often and recently decided to buy a house and live near him for a time. And so you met me in my guise as a schoolboy."

"That's what Basil's always working on, isn't it? A cure for you?"

"Yes, that and other things to help me. It is thanks to Basil that I'm spared many of the effects of my vampirism. I won't explain that now, but he's helped me a great deal. It is also thanks to Basil that you are not now a vampire yourself. What you drank the night I brought you here is a potion of his creation."

Josiah looked very worried, but I was too full of wonder at it all to do more than notice. Basil was Josiah's son? It was incredible. When I met Josiah, I sure never dreamed he had a son old enough to be my grandfather!

I wanted to hear more, and ask questions, but I could hardly keep my eyes open. I was so very tired that it was a strain just to listen. I drifted off asleep once again with one thought on my mind. There was still hope that Josiah could love me as more than a friend.

🍁　　　🍁　　　🍁

I awakened to find Basil gazing down at me with concern on his face. I had no idea how long I'd been asleep this time. I awakened now and then and I could never tell if minutes had passed, or days. Every time I awakened, I felt weaker. It was a struggle to even speak.

"I'm not getting any better, am I?" I asked him, although it was more of a statement than a question.

"It's very hard to tell, Graham. This is an entirely new area. No one really knows the full effects of the potion I gave you. I would not have done so without testing it, but we were out of options, and out of time."

"That potion, that's what you are working on all the time isn't it?" I asked him, although I already knew the answer. I'd never ventured to ask before, but things had changed. Things had changed in ways

I'd never imagined in my wildest dreams; Josiah was a vampire, so was Bry, and I'd nearly become one myself.

"Yes, and no," said Basil. "The potion I've been working on is not intended to prevent someone from becoming a vampire, it is to change a vampire back into a human. The potion I gave you is one of my many failures. It is a failure, however, that showed much promise. I knew that it could not change a vampire back into a human, but it did show signs that it could reverse the process if the transformation was not complete."

"And it does work, doesn't it? I'm not a vampire."

"No, you're not. Josiah and I tested you. You passed the tests and your body is free from all traces of vampirism."

"You're working on that potion for Josiah aren't you?" I said. Again, it was more statement than question.

"Yes, I've been working on it many, many long years. I've almost given up all hope many times, but I keep trying, keep searching for the right combination. The problem is that the possible herbal combinations are virtually infinite."

"Is there no way to cure a vampire then?" I asked.

"There is only one thing that stops a vampire from being a vampire, and that is removing his head. This does in fact "cure" him, but also kills the human within him. It is a fatal cure.

"The first vampire was created long, long ago by a curse. The reason is lost in the mists of time. The evil one who created the curse left but one way the curse could be lifted. It is as I have told you, the cure that kills. Once someone falls victim, there is no going back, there is no hope. Or at least very little hope."

CHAPTER 16

❀

The End and The Beginning

I struggled to open my eyes, but could not open them. The effort was too much. I had not the strength. I didn't know how much time had passed since I had last spoken to Josiah or Basil. It could have been minutes, or days, or weeks for all I knew. I could hear Basil and Josiah speaking in hushed voices. They were discussing something in earnest. As I listened, I knew that they were talking about me.

"He may yet come out of it," said Josiah. "There is still hope."

"There is always hope, Josiah, but you know as well as I that Graham grows ever weaker. A great deal of blood was drawn from him in a small amount of time when he was attacked and the potion that saved him from becoming a vampire has taxed his system to the breaking point. His body simply can't handle it. He is too weak and frail. There is only so much I can do. I've done all I can. We are losing him."

"Perhaps a hospital?"

"You know the answer to that already; less could be done for him there, than here."

I could hear Josiah crying. My heart felt for him. It was odd that I was thinking of him, while I lay there listening to them discuss me. I was dying and there was nothing anyone could do about it. Strangely, it didn't bother me as much as I would have thought. I was too tired to really care. I just wanted to rest…yes—rest.

"I don't want to lose him," said Josiah quietly "I'm so tired, tired of losing everyone I love. I've become so fond of Graham. I've grown to love him, Basil. I do love him. I love him in a way I've not loved anyone, not since Zachary. But now it's happening again. I don't think I can bear it this time, not again."

"There is a way to save him," said Basil quietly. There was a long, long pause.

"But how could I do that to him? How could I damn him to the same, lonely life that I have led?" There was nearly a pleading tone to Josiah's voice. He was tormented in mind and soul. I could hear him walk toward me. "Look at him, look at how young he is. It isn't fair that he should die so young. It isn't fair that he should miss out on so very much. We could have traveled the world together, seen so many wonderful things, but now…"

"You and he can still do all those things…" said Basil.

"But at what price?" I could tell that Josiah was tormented horribly. I could tell even Basil was uncertain about what he suggested. As I lay there, I was thinking about it a great deal myself. Death, or eternal life as a vampire?

Basil left the room and Josiah sat by my side, pushing my hair back off my forehead. He was weeping. It took me a few minutes to manage it, but I summoned all my strength, opened my eyes, and smiled at him weakly. He took my hand in his own.

I tried to speak, but I could not. I swallowed hard. Josiah lifted me up to a sitting position and gave me some water. He held me in his arms. There were tears in his eyes.

"It's okay, Josiah. I know I'm not getting better. I know I'm going to die. I don't think I'd even mind, but…" My voice wavered again, half from weakness, half from a sob welling in my throat. "I don't want to leave you, Josiah. I love you. I've never had a friend like you before. More than that...I love you. I want to stay with you."

Josiah's eyes filled with tears and they ran down his face. He looked away for a moment, and then back at me.

"There is a way you can stay, Graham. Basil suggested it, but I don't want to do that to you. I don't want to curse you with the life I lead."

"Tell me," I said weakly. I wanted to say more, that I'd overheard a great deal already, but it was too tiring. The few words I'd spoken had exhausted me.

"I can stop you from dying, if I take you. One bite on the neck is all it will take, but if I do it you will become like me. You will be a vampire, Graham. Once done, it cannot be undone. You will be doomed to an eternal life, to the loneliness and pain of eternity." He looked at me with pity, sadness, longing, and fear. The mix of his emotions was clear to read upon his features. He was unable to mask them. He felt them too keenly.

I wanted to speak, but I was fading. I could only keep my eyelids half open. It was too great a struggle to do more. I tried to speak, but could not. I wanted to tell him that I wanted to spend my life with him. I wanted to tell him that I was in love with him. I tried again and forced out a few halting words.

"I...don't......want...to leave you...Josiah." My mouth stayed half open and I was breathing hard from the effort of speaking. I could feel myself slipping away. I could feel myself begin to die.

"I want..." I said in a halting voice that was barely above a whisper. Josiah had to lean so close to hear me, even with his vampire ears, that his face was touching my own. "I want to...stay with....you. I love..."

I could say no more, my strength was gone. My head fell back and Josiah had to hold it up, for I was too weak to do so. I could feel myself slipping away more quickly. I knew that I was dying. It wasn't so bad really. I was so tired, I just wanted to rest. So tired...

Josiah leaned over me. I felt his hot breath on my neck. I felt his fangs as they pressed against my skin. I felt them sink into my neck and I felt him suck my blood. All went black, and I remembered nothing more.

※ ※ ※

I awakened with a start. I lay perfectly still, but my eyes popped wide open in an instant. Someone was sitting near me, crying. I could tell from the sobs that it was Josiah. My memory came flooding back to me. I'd been dying, laying in bed so weak I couldn't move, with darkness coming upon me, then Josiah had sank his fangs into my neck and I knew no more.

I'd been so very sick and weak, but now I felt well and strong. I sat up. I felt stronger than I ever had in my life. All my senses were far keener than they had ever been. I could see with perfect clarity. I could read the tiny print on books all the way across the room. I could hear more clearly too. I could hear a little bird digging for worms outside, and I could hear more. All my senses had expanded. It was overwhelming.

Josiah was in such a state of grief that he had not noticed me sit up. When he did, he jumped to his feet.

"Graham," he said, peering at me. I smiled at him.

"Graham, you shouldn't sit up."

"I'm fine," I said. "I'm perfectly fine."

I felt my neck. All the marks were gone. There were healed as if they'd never been. Josiah was still looking at me, looking at me as if he were grieving over my death.

"I'm sorry, Graham," he said.

"Sorry for what?"

"Sorry for making you into a creature such as myself. Sorry for damning you to living an eternal life of loneliness. Sorry for throwing you into the pain of eternity."

"But I won't be lonely, Josiah. Don't you see? I'll always have you. Death will take those I love away from me, and it will be hard, but that is life. Even mortal souls must deal with that. It is inescapable. All I've ever wanted was one good, true friend, and now I have you. I won't be alone, and neither will you, Josiah. You said I reminded you of your Zachary, maybe I'm even Zachary come back to be your friend again. Whether or not, it doesn't matter, because I am your friend. I'm here, and I will always be. You are the friend I've always needed and wanted. And I'm the friend that you've always longed for, too. You'll never be alone again, Josiah. I'm a friend that will never die."

Josiah hugged me. He was crying still, but I knew that he was happy. He'd been the most lonely creature in all the world, but he'd never be lonely again.

🍁　　　🍁　　　🍁

Josiah and I sat and talked quietly. It was all we could do since he wouldn't let me get out of bed. Suddenly, my face fell; I realized something. I was a vampire. What if I wasn't a vampire like Josiah? What if I was a vampire like Bry and all the others? There was much more to it than not having a reflection in the mirror.

"Josiah, will I…will I have to drink blood? I don't want to drink blood. I don't even like drinking milk." I was beginning to get upset with the thought of it, and with worse things. "What if I turn into something evil? What if I go around killing people, the way Bry has? I can't do that, Josiah, I can't!"

Josiah held me in his arms and petted my hair. I was frightened, more than I'd ever been before. My whole life had become an unknown. I felt like I wasn't even myself anymore.

"Graham, listen to me. Let's take this one step at a time, okay? I know it's frightening. I know there are lots of things you don't understand. I'll be here with you through it all, okay? I'm not going anywhere. You aren't alone in this." I hugged him and cried onto his shoulder.

"Josiah, I don't want to be like Bry. I can't stand the thought of hurting anyone. I don't want to be like that."

"We will know the full extent of what has happened to you soon enough."

"When? How long before I know if I'll have to drink blood?" I asked.

"We will know that when you get hungry."

"I'm already hungry," I said.

It was mid-afternoon. Despite my protests that I felt fine, Josiah and Basil insisted that I rest. We talked as the hours slipped by and my hunger grew more intense. Basil said that by nightfall, we'd have the answer to the question that scared me the most. As the shadows began to lengthen, my fear increased. I didn't know what I'd do if I turned out to be a creature like Bry.

"Josiah…"

"Yes?"

"If I…if I'm like Bry. Don't let me hurt anyone, okay? If I start to become…evil, I want you to do what you have to do, okay? I don't want to live like that. You've given me a chance to live when I would have died, but I don't want to live if others must die so that I can survive. Promise me you'll do what needs to be done. Promise me."

I knew I was hurting Josiah. Tears had come to his eyes. I knew that if he had to kill me, he'd be killing the only friend who could be with him always. He'd be destroying what he wanted the most in all the world.

"Promise me?"

"I…I can't, Graham. I just can't."

I wanted to plead with him, but I understood. His refusal frightened me, however. If I was one them, a full vampire, there was no turning back.

"Vampires aren't really evil, you know," said Josiah. "Even though they kill to survive, even though they feed on the fear of others. They are just creatures like the rest of us. They do what they have to do."

"How can you say that? Just think of that boy that Bry killed. Regular people don't do that."

"All of us survive on the death of others," said Josiah.

"No. We don't."

"But we do. When you eat a hamburger, where do you think that meat comes from? When you have eggs for breakfast, or fried chicken for supper, an animal has to die so that you can live. Even vegetables are killed when they are harvested, although we don't think of it that way. We all survive on the death of others, so don't judge vampires too harshly."

I had never thought of it that way. I guess to a chicken, I was every bit as bad as a vampire already.

Josiah went on. "Some vampires do kill for pleasure; Bry is one of those, but most are just like you and me and mortal souls—they kill to survive. Most people don't see things that way because they have others do the killing for them. They go to the grocery and buy steaks, hamburgers, fish, and poultry all neatly cut up and packaged. They are just as responsible for the deaths, however, as surely as if they'd done the killing themselves."

I didn't like what Josiah was saying, but it was true. It was a very harsh way to look at things, but it was reality; a reality no one liked to think about. Despite Josiah's words, I was ravenously hungry. Basil was frying chicken for our supper and it smelled delicious. Even though I knew that chicken had been killed so that we could eat it, I still wanted it. I craved it. I was so hungry my stomach was aching. It made me understand what Josiah was saying. I wasn't evil for wanting that chicken. Vampires weren't evil either. We just saw them as evil because they preyed upon us. Where vampires were concerned, we were the chickens.

Josiah was watching me intently, observing.

"I think it's time to eat," he said. His eyes locked on mine and I felt self-conscious. "Are you hungry, Graham?"

"Starving!"

"And what is it you are starving for?"

"Well, that chicken smells sooo good."

"Chicken? Not blood?"

"No!"

Josiah smiled.

"Then, I would say you've passed the test. If you needed the blood of others to survive, you would crave it by now so strongly that I'd have to fight you to keep you from going out into the night."

I let out a huge sigh of relief. I felt like a tremendous weight had been lifted from my shoulders. Josiah hugged me.

"So…" I said, "let's eat!"

I was so hungry that my stomach ached. I felt all shaky as I sat down. The fried chicken, mashed potatoes, corn, freshly baked rolls, and everything else looked so delicious that I felt I could eat every bit of it myself.

"Oh, man!" I said, as we sat devouring fried chicken.

"What is it?"

"What am I going to tell my parents? It's not like I can just slip it into a conversation or something—*Oh, by the way, I'm a vampire now.*"

"You need not tell them anything," said Josiah, "at least not yet."

"But what happens when they find out I don't have a reflection in mirrors? What happens when they start asking why I don't stay out in the sun anymore?"

"We can hide all that from them, Graham. I've hidden myself for centuries and none, but you, have discovered my secret."

I knew he was speaking the truth, but I still wondered how we'd pull it off. I wondered about my parents too. I was going back home. I'd already decided that. Whether I'd stay or not remained to be seen.

I didn't want to think about that for the moment; I was too busy enjoying being alive.

CHAPTER 17

Homecoming

My mother dropped the clean laundry basket on the floor and ran to me as I entered the house, spilling towels and washcloths everywhere. She clasped me in a hug so tight I thought she'd squeeze the life right out of me.

"Graham! Graham! I've been so worried! I've missed you so much! Where have you been? We've searched for you for days!"

She covered my face with kisses and mussed my hair. She kept holding me by the shoulders looking at me, then pulling me to her to hug me again. I didn't mind—she loved me.

My dad entered the room. I eyed him suspiciously. The last time I'd seen him, he'd slapped me in the face for being gay. I saw something as I looked at him that I'd never seen before. It was something that tugged at my heart and set my mind at ease; Dad was crying.

He ran to me and hugged me tightly, too. He ran his fingers through my hair, then hugged me again. He kissed my cheeks and forehead and hugged me some more.

"I'm sorry!" he said. "I'm so sorry, Graham. I'm sorry I hit you. I'm sorry I said what I did. I'm sorry I wasn't a better father."

He actually cried on my shoulder. It made me cry too.

When my parents were done kissing and hugging me, I stepped back and stared at them with a level gaze.

"I'm not going to that center," I stated flatly. "I'm gay and that's all there is to it. I couldn't change if I wanted to and I don't want to. I'm not going to that place. If you try to send me, I'll run away again, and this time I won't come back."

It felt strange delivering an ultimatum to my parents, but I meant every word. I wasn't going. If they tried to force me, I'd have Josiah to help me escape. If they tried to make me go, they'd lose me forever.

"You don't have to go," said my dad. "While you were gone, I checked into that place. I'd never send you there!"

Mom made all my favorites for supper; homemade pepperoni pizza, breadsticks, applesauce, and chocolate cake with ice-cream and chocolate syrup for dessert. After we'd eaten, we sat around the table and talked and talked, about a lot of things, but mostly about me being gay and how they loved me no matter what. Were these the same parents I had when I'd run away? It almost seemed like they'd been replaced while I was gone. I almost couldn't believe the change in them, but I was glad of it nonetheless.

I didn't breathe a word to my parents about being a vampire—like they'd believe something like that! I'd have to tell them eventually, but not just yet. I wondered how they'd react when I told them at last.

🍁   🍁   🍁

I felt odd…changed. That wasn't surprising in the least. I was changed—drastically changed. I might look like the same frail boy I'd always been, but I was vastly different in ways that eyes could not see.

One difference was most unpleasant. At each corner of my bed was a small bunch of lemon balm. As a test, I slowly reached out, drawing my fingers near it, without touching. I remembered well how Josiah's skin had blistered from it. When my fingers were nearly upon it, I felt them begin to burn, as if I were holding them much too close to a fire. I withdrew my hand quickly.

I took a pair of long scissors and cut each bunch of lemon balm loose, except that near my window. I used a broom and a dustpan to gather it up with a minimum of discomfort. I was relieved when I dumped it into the trash in the kitchen.

I wondered how I would protect myself now. I could no longer wear a small bag of lemon balm around my neck as I had done. I was a vampire now too and it would harm me as much as the others. At least no vampire would come through my window.

I wondered about Bry. Where had he gone? Was he still intent on destroying me? Josiah had not talked about it, but I wondered if he'd taken care of Bry already. I gulped when I thought of what he might have done.

I was different. On my first night at home, it was my eyes that I noticed; they were more keen and bright. The biggest change was not their appearance; I could now see in the dark just as well as I could in the light. Instead of dimness and shadows, I saw everything as if every nook and cranny were lit by bright moonlight. There were no shadows for me. Darkness had ceased to be darkness. No wonder I'd never heard of a vampire that carried a flashlight.

I found myself wishing I could tell my parents about the changes in my life, but how could I tell them something they'd find so unbelievable? I knew, without doubt, that vampires were real, but my parents would likely think I was just plain crazy. I might as well have told them I'd been changed into an elf or a leprechaun.

They would have to find out eventually. Like Josiah before me, I would not change with the passing of time. I'd be thirteen forever. Within a year, if not before, my parents would notice my lack of growth. The more time that passed, the more it would be obvious that I wasn't growing older. I'd have to tell my parents then. It would be best to wait. I'd let them see for themselves that time didn't touch me, then explain to them why. With obvious evidence before them, it would be much easier to believe.

I grew a little sad as I thought about the changes that would not take place. I would never grow any taller. I'd never get hair on my chest. I'd always be small, and young. I'd be always a boy—never a man.

Was that really so bad, though? My parents were always saying I should enjoy being a kid because it was a time that would never come again. For me, it was a time that would never end. So what if I could never grow hair on my upper lip or chin? Dad said it was a real pain to shave all the time anyway. Most people dreamed of being young forever. I had that. Wasn't never growing up worth that price? I could be a kid forever. I was Peter Pan.

I couldn't help but be a little sad about never growing up. After all, I'd been looking forward to it for quite some time. Maybe it would be okay, however. Whether or not I liked it, facts were facts. I was a vampire and would forever be thirteen. The best I could do was enjoy it.

I thought back to the night I'd tried to kill myself. It was ironic in a way. The boy who wanted to do himself in was now immortal. Not only would I live the span of a normal life, but also I'd live far, far beyond it, unless someone like Bry managed to separate my head from my body.

The night I'd nearly killed myself was the first time I'd met Josiah too, even though I didn't know it then. I had no idea as I approached the lonely boy, sitting all alone in the cafeteria, that I'd already met him. In fact, he'd already saved my life. If he hadn't frightened me into dumping all those pills in the mud, I'd have killed myself for sure. That wasn't the last time he saved me either. And now, he'd made me immortal. Truth was definitely stranger than fiction.

I felt weird as I walked into school on Monday. It was my first day back in many days. I looked at everything with new eyes. I had a whole different perspective on life. I didn't get upset when I had trouble with math. I literally had forever to understand it. It didn't matter how long it took, I could learn it. There wasn't anything I wouldn't be able to learn or accomplish. I had an endless lifetime to do it all.

I no longer felt timid and afraid. I was the same size as always, but I knew I could take care of myself. I was already growing stronger. I'd been a vampire only a short time and already I was sure I was as strong as most of the boys in my class. I hadn't expected my strength to increase quite so quickly. Josiah told me it took him quite a while to notice he was getting stronger. Maybe it was because I was so weak to begin with. Josiah was already strong from working in the fields when he'd been made into a vampire. I was just a skinny, little weakling. Maybe my strength increased faster because I had so very far to go, or maybe I just recognized what was going on more quickly because I knew it was coming.

I laughed to myself. I'd always been the puny one, but no more. As the years passed, my strength would grow. Someday, I'd be stronger than everyone. Who would have guessed it, me, the little runt, the strongest of all?

When gym class rolled around I didn't dread it like I normally did. Calisthenics were a breeze. I could do pushups almost without trying and I could do sit-ups as if I had abs of steel. I still sucked at playing soccer, but I knew I could do it if I tried. If I wanted to put the time into it, I could be the best there ever was. I could do anything!

At lunchtime, I sneaked into the weight room that the football team used for working out. It was deserted. I tried the bench press. The best I could ever do before was thirty pounds. How pathetic. I put on fifty pounds and I could lift it! I tried sixty pounds and I could do it too. I couldn't quite handle seventy-five pounds, but I came close. I couldn't believe it, I could bench press sixty pounds when I'd only been able to bench thirty in the past. I was twice as strong as I was before!

I felt more confident than ever. The kids around me and even the teachers seemed to pick up on it. They seemed to look at me differently somehow. Maybe it was my imagination, but I felt like they respected me now.

I'd thought that Josiah had killed Bry, but I saw him at school on my first day back. The way Bry looked at me made my skin crawl. He couldn't turn me into a vampire, because I already was one, but he could still kill me and I was sure he'd do it in a very nasty way if he got the chance. I was not invulnerable. I was a new vampire and very, very weak by vampire standards. Even Bry's natural strength was beyond mine, and his strength as a vampire far, far exceeded my own. If he got the chance, Bry could rip my head off with ease. When he looked at me with his cold eyes, it gave me a chill.

❦ ❦ ❦

It was mere days before Bry and I came face to face. I left Basil's house just before dusk and walked to the end of the lane where I usually met Josiah. I started to speak to him as I neared when I realized it wasn't Josiah at all.

"Hello, Graham. We have some unfinished business to settle," said Bry.

I looked around, but Josiah was nowhere in sight. I was worried.

"Looking for someone? Oh yes, Josiah. He's been…detained." Bry grinned evilly.

"If you've hurt him, I'll…"

"You'll what? You think you're tough now, do you Graham? I'll show you how tough you aren't! Right before I snuff out your puny existence, I'll show you. You don't deserve to be one of us!"

I did the only thing I knew to do. I ran. I turned and bolted back the way I had come. I was even faster than I had been as a boy, but Bry was faster still. He would have grabbed me if I wasn't so adept at dodging out of reach. All those years of running from the terrible twins had taught me a thing or two.

Just as I reached Basil's door, I heard a terrible commotion behind me. Josiah had come out of nowhere and flung himself on Bry. Wherever he'd been, he was back. Whatever Bry had done to keep him away, it hadn't worked for long.

Josiah and Bry were rolling on the ground, each determined to kill the other, but neither could, for both were immortal. It was a terrible fight to see. I felt that I should join in and aid Josiah, but I knew I was far less powerful than either of them. Likely, I'd only get in Josiah's way.

"Basil!" I yelled, as I watched in horror as Bry threw Josiah to the ground.

Josiah was not there when Bry dropped to land on him, however, he'd already rolled away and jumped to his feet. The two of them clashed and were locked in a deadly fight, fingers around each other's necks. When they released each other, it was to deliver deadly blows. If they were mere mortals, the blows they each received would have killed them.

Josiah slammed Bry into a post on the porch so hard it cracked and the roof began to sag. I was afraid the whole porch would come crashing down upon us all. There was another crack as Josiah broke a bit of the porch railing away. Bry fought like mad to escape. He pounded on Josiah's arms, but Josiah kept him pinned to the post with one hand wrapped around his throat. Josiah drew the splintered wood from the railing back and plunged the stake at Bry's heart.

"Stop!" yelled Basil.

I had not even noticed him step unto the porch, but there he was. He spoke with such authority that Josiah froze in mid-stab. He brought the stake to halt at the last possible second. The tip was poised against Bry's heart. Had Josiah thrust it through him, it would not have killed him, but Bry's death would not have been long in coming. With Bry incapacitated, Josiah could have easily removed his head.

"Bring him inside," said Basil.

I had no idea what Basil was doing, but I trusted him without reservation. Bry seemed to fear him beyond reason. Josiah twisted Bry's arm behind his back and led him inside. I stepped out of the way, then followed.

Josiah shoved Bry into a chair and held him there. Bry hissed at him, but didn't put up much of a struggle. I think he knew he didn't stand a chance of escaping from Josiah as long as he was holding him down.

"Step away," said Basil quietly.

Josiah looked at him, as if he doubted the wisdom of doing so, but he did as Basil said. Basil took his place and stood before Bry with a smoking flask in his hand. Bry snarled at him, baring his fangs, but made no move toward him. Basil's presence was overwhelming. Such power exuded from him that I almost couldn't believe he was the same kindly man who paid me so much to run errands for him.

"Drink this," he said to Bry, holding the flask out to him.

To my complete surprise, Bry obeyed. He upended the flask and drained it in one gulp. I looked at him, but nothing seemed to happen. I had little doubt that it was another of Basil's attempts at a cure, but as none had yet been successful, I had little hope for it.

When something happened at last, it was a small, almost imperceptible event. Bry did not writhe in the chair, his face contorting. There was no flash of smoke. It seemed almost as if nothing happened at all, but then I noticed his bared fangs growing shorter. At first, I wasn't even sure it had happened, but as I watched, it became evident. Bry's prominent fangs slowly shortened until they were no longer than the usual canines. Basil and Josiah looked at each other, a look of wonder on their features.

"And now for the real test," said Basil.

He produced a small bunch of newly cut lemon balm. Both Josiah and I took a step backward. Bry looked at it in great fear. He leaned back as Basil brought it forward. He trembled as Basil touched his face. A look of surprise came over his features. Bry caressed his cheek as if astounded that he was unharmed.

Basil stepped back and gestured toward the mirror. Bry slowly stood and stepped to the looking glass.

"I can see myself," he said.

We all joined him in peering into the mirror. It was just as he'd said. We could see him. Bry was cured. He was a vampire no more.

Relief was evident on Josiah's face. He had no desire to kill Bry, or anyone. He only sought to destroy Bry to keep him from killing. Bry himself was in total shock. It was almost as if he couldn't believe what had happened. He looked around at us and gave Basil a slight smile. He took Basil's hands in his own, and kissed them.

I gazed at Bry. Maybe it was just that I knew he was no longer a vampire, but he seemed changed. He seemed...nicer. He was just an ordinary football jock now and no longer a creature of the night. I found myself wondering how old he really was. Was he in his late teens? Or was he hundreds of years old like Josiah? Someday, I'd have to ask him. Bry thanked Basil, then walked out of the house in a bit of a daze. No one tried to stop him. There was no longer any need.

"You did it!" said Josiah.

"We should give this to everyone Bry has made into a vampire," I said, excitement evident in my voice.

"Un-necessary," said Basil. "As soon as Bry ceased to be a vampire, so did they."

"You mean there are no vampires around here anymore?" I asked.

"Only two," said Basil, and smiled.

Basil turned to his stove and filled a small flask of the bubbling liquid for Josiah.

"Be careful. It's hot. Let it cool."

Josiah could not wait. He had waited for centuries already and couldn't bear even a few minutes more. He held the flask out in front of him and I feared he'd down it, whether or not it burned his throat. He let it cool a bit though, then drank it in one, long draught.

Josiah, Basil, and I all stood there as the minutes ticked away. Bry's fangs had receded within just a few moments, but Josiah's were still there. Mine were too. I had not drank the potion, but if Josiah was cured, I would be as well. He'd made me into a vampire and what he'd done would be undone if he ceased to be a vampire himself.

I began to fear that something was wrong. Josiah and I looked into the mirror. Our faces did not peer back at us. I could clearly the see the room around us, but we were invisible.

"It didn't work, did it?" I asked.

"No."

"But it worked for Bry."

"I'm different. Something about me is keeping it from working."

Josiah sat down, dejected. I knew what hopes he had for the potion to change him back into a real boy. He'd been waiting for hundreds of years, and now, just when hope was the brightest, he'd failed.

"I'm sorry, Josiah," I told him. He looked at me with tears in his eyes. It wasn't long before he broke down and cried. It was my turn to comfort him, as he had comforted me so many times. I put my arm around his shoulders and held him. I let him cry himself out.

"Maybe it's better this way," I said. "My mom always says that everything happens for a reason. Everything happens just as it's supposed to happen. Maybe we aren't meant to be cured. Maybe we're meant to be vampires."

"We're meant to suffer? We're meant to see everyone we love die? You know it will happen sooner or later. You haven't experienced it yet, but you will."

"I'd have to face the death of those I love even if I wasn't a vampire. The only difference is that now I know it will happen for sure. I don't want to lose my parents. I don't want to lose anyone, but that's the way life is and I can't change it. And besides, you are forgetting one very important thing. We each have one friend who we'll never lose. We each have one friend that will be there forever. We have each other."

Josiah smiled at that.

"Having you as my friend might just make it bearable," he said. "I still don't understand why we're meant to be vampires."

"Well, Basil's just came up with a cure. It's going to take a very, very long time to track down every last vampire and give him the potion. Who but an immortal could do it? Maybe that's our purpose in life. Think about it. That potion wouldn't even exist if it wasn't for you. Basil made it to cure you. It won't work for you, or me, but it will work for all the others. Think of all the suffering that will come to an end because of Basil, and because of you. Think of all the people that won't have to die now, because the vampires will be cured. Think of the vampires themselves, who will now be able to return to what they were. People dream of finding a cure for cancer and AIDS. Isn't this just as important?"

"Yeah, I guess you're right."

"Even if I'm not, it doesn't matter. Even if all this is some kind of fluke, we were given our lives to live. This is the hand we were dealt. We can either mope around and feel sorry for ourselves, or we can enjoy it. There is so much to do, so much to see, so much to learn and explore. The whole world is out there waiting for us and we've got forever to see it all. We'll be young and strong forever. Who could ask for anything more?"

I looked over at Basil. Our eyes met for a few lingering moments. Basil excused himself and went outside. I think he knew I had something very private to tell Josiah.

"There's something more," I said, then grew silent. It was suddenly very hard to speak.

"What is it?" asked Josiah.

"I have a confession. I, uh…I think of you as more than a friend."

I closed my eyes for a moment. Why couldn't I just say it? After all I'd been through, after all I'd faced, why was this so hard? I opened my eyes back up and Josiah was gazing at me intently, a slight smile playing on the edges of his mouth.

"I don't just love you…I'm in love with you, Josiah," I managed at last.

Tears welled up in Josiah's eyes. He was crying.

"I don't know how you feel about me," I began, with my head lowered "but…"

"I love you," said Josiah.

I jerked my head up and looked at him.

"I love you," he repeated.

I smiled at him, rushed to him, and hugged him tight. I was so happy that I cried too. Josiah leaned back, took my head in his hands, and kissed me on the lips. It was my very first kiss and the most wonderful feeling in all the world.

"I love you," I told him again. "And you don't have to worry about losing me like all the others. It doesn't matter if we live a thousand times ten thousand years, we'll always be together. Neither of us ever has to be lonely again.

The End

About the Author

In addition to "The Vampire's Heart", Mark A. Roeder is also the author of "Gay Youth Chronicles", a series of books about gay youth, centered in Indiana. Information on his current and upcoming books can be found at markroeder.com. Those wishing to contact him may reach him at **markaroeder@yahoo.com**.

0-595-22564-0